THE
44 RULES
OF
AMATEUR SLEUTHING

by Jamie Nash

The 44 Rules of Amateur Sleuthing

http://www.jamienash.net
© 2018 Jamie Nash

jamie.nash@verizon.net

Cover Art by Greg Rebis
Book Design by Susan Mangan

Paperback ISBN: 978-0-9990913-9-5

For Luke, who stayed up with me every night
to write and drink formula.

...and just to be clear, he was drinking the formula.

Amateur Sleuth Rule #1

Crime has no curfew...
but it tends to sleep in.

BOOM-BOOM-BA-BOOM-BOOM. A thunderous pounding tested the foundation of the house. It shook the comic-posters that hung behind Mandrake Mandrake's bed. It rattled the twelve-year-old's shelf of stuffed animals and jolted his favorite magnifying glass off his desk.

BOOM-BOOM. Mandrake detected a musicality in the earth-rattling wallops. A song. Shave. And. A. Hair. Cut. Two-bits.

Someone was knocking on Mandrake's front door. Only one man knocked like that.

Crash Brickfist.

Mandrake scrambled down the stairs and peered into the living room. His ancient grandmother lounged in her customary flower-print chair, needles chittering in her lap. There's no way she could've missed that pounding. It probably rattled her dentures out. But she said nothing and didn't look up. Good. If she knew the world's most rough and tumble private eye was banging down her door after supper time, Mandrake would have some serious explaining to do. Better to keep this visit on the down-low.

Mandrake slinked into the foyer and eased the front door open. On the porch, a massive, trench-coated figure blotted out the lights of the city. The man's back was to the door, watching the street.

Grab your jacket, kid," the private eye's voice rumbled like a South Pacific volcano. "The Bearded Bank Bandit has struck again."

"You can't be here, Crash." Mandrake's teeth chattered. The chill night air cut through his snoring giraffe pajamas. Still, the boy didn't dare invite the refrigerator-sized palooka into the warm house. If Grandma got wind that he was palling around with one of the city's greatest crime-busters, frigid temperatures would be the least of his troubles.

"We got six bank vaults, empty as a pauper's pocketbook." Crash's sleepy yet never-closing eyes peered out beneath the brim of his fedora watching the street, always on the lookout. "Chief Doyle's rounding up the suspects. We need to end this thing. Tonight.»

"I can't, Crash." Mandrake shuffled his pajama-footied feet. "It's a school night."

Crash turned, glacier slow, like an ocean liner in a fedora with an unlit cigar hanging off its bow. The scar tissue that passed for eyebrows in his granite-etched face rose almost a millimeter.

"I have an important test tomorrow." Mandrake shrugged. "There's no way Grandma's going to let me come out. Not tonight." Mandrake glanced toward the living room where Grandma's afghan-covered feet poked into view.

"Let me have a word." Crash cracked the knuckles of his left ham-hock-sized hand. "I'm a good convincer."

"That's my grandmother, Crash."

Crash ducked through the doorway. "I'll be gentle."

"You'll have to take off your shoes and hat before you come inside."

Crash fixed Mandrake with a glare that could melt a Frogurt Franchise.

"Grandma's house." Mandrake gulped. "Grandma's rules."

Crash kicked off his gunboat shoes, hung his fedora on the coat rack, and followed Mandrake into the doily and knick-knack-laden living room.

Grandma didn't bother to look up.

"Ma'am," Crash socked feet sunk into the shag carpet. "I'd like to borrow the kid."

"On a school night?" Grandma slid her white Home-Alert wrist watch deep beneath her sleeve. Perhaps her heart skipped a beat at the mere suggestion of her tweener grandson gallivanting out after curfew or maybe she was considering punching Crash in his cinder block jaw.

"It's a matter of great importance, ma'am."

"Life and death, I presume?" Grandma asked.

"I wouldn't have taken off my fedora if it wasn't."

"And how could a child help with such matters?"

"He's a boy with exceptional talents."

"Hmf. Have you seen his report card?"

"Report cards aren't my beat."

"His marks in seventh grade Latin are less than ideal. Mandrake needs foreign language credits to get into art school."

Crash groaned. "Art school?"

Mandrake shrugged. "I like to draw."

"Until his grades are up to snuff," Grandma continued, "there will be no extracurricular nonsense."

"What if Crash helps me study?" Mandrake said. "Like a study-buddy."

Grandma raised a brow. "Am I to believe Mr. Brickfist is an expert in the Romance languages?"

"Only enough to order pizza," Crash said.

"He can quiz me," Mandrake countered.

Crash crinkled his brow. "Um... maybe we can work in a few flashcards between interrogations."

Mandrake nodded. "Grandma, you read the papers. You've heard about the Bearded Bank Bandit. This is important. Not just to me but the entire city."

Crash picked up. "Kid's right. If this crime-spree goes on, banks will crash. People will lose their savings."

Grandma raised her bloodshot eyes to Crash. "You know what

happens when you start a boy down this path. You know how it can end up?"

Crash lowered his voice, lullaby-soft. "This kid isn't his father. He won't make the same mistakes."

"And I suppose," Grandma said, "that you're an expert judge of character?"

"That's half the job, ma'am."

"And the other half?"

"The other half I don't let the kid tangle in."

"No." Grandma stood up. "It's out of the question."

Crash grabbed her arm. "Can we talk alone? It's important."

They both turned to Mandrake.

"Oh, I'll just wait in the closet." Mandrake backpedaled to the foyer, squeezed inside with the coats and shoes and shut the door. Darkness swallowed him. But he wasn't completely sealed off from the private conversation. He caught bits and pieces.

First Grandma, "Letting a boy play in a man's world is dangerous —"

Then Crash: "You know what's at stake!"

Then some intense whispering. Mostly Grandma. Crash was tough, but Grandma was "Grandma tough." There was zero chance she'd allow her only grandson to go off and solve crimes with this rough-and-tumble gumshoe was ludicrous. She only recently granted him 'cross the street without holding hands privileges'. She still didn't allow him to operate the microwave.

The door suddenly ripped open. Crash loomed over him.

"Come on kid, we've got a crime to solve."

Mandrake's jaw dropped. "She said I could go? What did you do to her?"

"We just talked. Need-to-know stuff." Crash shoved his feet into his loafers and slapped on his Fedora. "But if you don't pass that Latin test we're both gonna need witness protection."

Amateur Sleuth Rule #2

Vomit can ruin a crime scene.
Have a vomit strategy.

"The coppers staked out six of the twelve Capital City banks tonight," Crash climbed out of his sleek black supercharger. "The other six were the ones hit. This one was the biggest."

Awash in red and blue lights, Mandrake peered over the clutter of crookedly parked police cruisers to the large brick building.

Crash lifted a barricade of yellow tape emblazoned with black letters that read — "POLICE LINE DON'T CROSS."

Mandrake hesitated. "This is my first crime scene."

Crash smiled and cocked his head in a far-off stare. "I remember my first. Double homicide. Lots of blood. Lots of guts. The good old days."

Mandrake's stomach gurgled. He nervously spied the glut of cops and detectives and grim-faced reporters. "I wish I wore more professional pajamas. Like ones with rocket-ships or superheroes."

"Don't worry about these goons," Crash grunted. "Just focus on the case. Whadda we got on the Bearded Bandit?"

Mandrake swiped his phone and navigated to his notes. "We know from the security footage that he wears a disguise."

A black and white security video leaked to local news captured images of a man, his face shrouded in a costume-shop purchased black mountain-man beard that hung to his waist, where the striped casing of a king-sized pillow jutted out from his bursting-at-the-seams jacket.

"If it's a disguise, why always the same one?" Crash began walking toward the bank, squeezing through the cars and first-responders.

Mandrake followed closely, skimming his notes. "He's not trying to hide his identity. He's trying to establish one."

"Because... ?"

"He wants us to know it was him."

"Personal glory?"

"...or misdirection? Maybe the disguise is a trick. What if there's an army of these bandits, all wearing the exact same get-up?"

"My gut says this mug's a solo operator."

Mandrake spied the crime scene investigation crew, who swept the windows with their science kits, dusting for prints and shining their large fluorescent lights. "They're wasting their time. He never leaves clues."

"That dices no onions with me." Crash trotted up the steps and toward the bank's front door. "Anybody who watches enough cop shows knows how to leave a crime scene spotless."

"Maybe. But you don't learn to crack a bank vault by watching TV. Not even on cable."

"That narrows it a little. I hear Valentine Velvet is out of the women's slammer. She can open any safe with a salt shaker and two ball-point pens."

"She's only been out of prison for a month." Mandrake flicked to his phone's calendar. "The Bandit has been at this for longer than that."

"She wouldn't look good in a beard, anyway," Crash mused.

"There's something else." Mandrake focused on today's date. "The thefts have all occurred between the hours of seven and nine pm. And always on Mondays. It's got to mean something."

Crash stopped at the door. "Look kid, before we go in, there are some ground rules."

Mandrake nodded and opened the notes app to jot them down.

"First off, never leave my side. No matter what."

Mandrake typed it in.

"And if your nerves get the best of you, don't vomit on the evidence."

"Right," Mandrake typed , Barfing Bad. "I'll do my best but sometimes it's just... blaaaah!"

"And most importantly, if anyone needs to be punched, shot or judo chopped, you assume the position, okay? Curled up in a corner or under a desk, head between the knees, eyes closed, and ears covered."

"Ears, Crash?"

"Sometimes during a beat-down the beat-ee's language can get a little age-inappropriate."

They pushed through the revolving door into the large marble lobby toward a team of detectives that lingered by the open vault.

A couple of cops from the 87th Precinct smirked. "Nice giraffes, junior."

Mandrake blushed. "My trench coat is at the cleaners."

"Brickfist!" A hunched troll of a man with a nest of tangled neck hair like some deranged Santa Claus yelled across the hall and swiped a teal bowling ball bag in the detective's direction. "The Private Eye game must really be slowing down if you have to take up baby-sitting as a side-gig."

Crash groaned. "This is no side-gig, Chief. This is —"

"Mandrake Mandrake." The bearded bowler sneered. "I know the brat. All too well."

Mandrake ducked behind Crash. "Maybe I should wait in the car."

"Why are you even here, Brickfist?" The Chief picked at his bloated belly between the buttons of his strained-to-the limits bowling shirt then sniffed his finger. "What's your angle?"

"Same as usual, Chief. Banks hired me to do the job the coppers can't."

"I don't have time for either of you clowns tonight." The Chief stormed ahead brushing Mandrake with his heavy bowling ball bag.

Crash and Mandrake followed Doyle up the marble staircase and into the bank's elegant boardroom.

The Chief squeezed around the leather chairs and plopped down at the far-side of the long conference table. "I left the middle of my seventh frame for this. I was bowling a two-forty. It would have been my high-score."

"Two-forty?" Mandrake questioned.

"That's right. What's it to you?" Doyle slid his bag under the table like he was handling a delicate family heirloom. "You a bowler?"

Mandrake shook his head. "More of a skee-baller. Not professionally or anything."

Doyle laid out a folder stuffed with police reports. "Well, this is an adults-only crime scene. I'll call you when we've got a case concerning hand puppets or candy-colored singing dinosaurs."

Mandrake clenched his teeth. Crash warned him he'd get no respect until he started shaving. But it still irked him.

Crash sunk down in a chair, leaned back, and kicked his size 18's up on the mahogany table. "The kid's helped you out of jams before, Chief. In fact, he's the reason you're Chief at all."

Before Crash and Mandrake teamed-up, Mandrake spent his mornings solving mysteries from his breakfast nook over a bowl of Cocoa Banana Loops and a glass of grapefruit juice. The boy's 'Nose' was so attuned that merely reading second-hand accounts of burglaries, murders and break-ins in the Daily Capital's crime-blotter provided enough clues to crack cases that eluded teams of professional crime busters.

During his bus rides to school, Mandrake emailed his conclusions to the Police Tip Line. Typically, his expertise was rewarded with a form response that read something along the lines of "don't call us, we'll call you."

Officer Doyle — he wasn't chief then – worked the tip-line, a low level job given to the most inept of cops. Until he began secretly using Mandrake's tips.

"I know all about the Case of the Mysterious Mimic." Brickfist pointed a finger at the Chief.

The Mimic was Capital City's most notorious serial bank robber. He had an uncanny ability to recreate precisely the look and sound of the city's wealthiest citizens which he'd use to loot their safe deposit boxes, trusted bank employees standing right beside them and never noticing a thing. He'd been captured after a story appeared in the newspaper about Queen La of the Kingdom of Opar coming to visit, and taking out a box at First Capital City Trust. When the Mimic showed up in royal African mufti, it was easy to figure out who he was — there is no Kingdom of Opar. Mandrake had planted the story in the paper himself and alerted the tip-line.

Doyle made the bust and pretended the whole thing was his idea.

"We both know how you got promoted to chief." Crash cocked his head at Doyle. "You know how good the kid is. You've been stealing his thunder for long enough. Give him a chance."

"You been telling tales, kid?!!" Doyle's hot red face turned to Mandrake. "Do you remember what I told you the last time we spoke?!"

Mandrake shuddered. Months ago, he'd confronted Doyle at police headquarters and promised never to reveal the secret behind Doyle's meteoric rise, if Doyle would just give him access to actual evidence, reports, and crime scenes.

The Chief threw him out and threatened that if Mandrake ever hinted he was secretly behind Doyle's success, Mandrake would spend the rest of his prepubescent years in juvenile hall.

Luckily, sitting in police headquarters that night, Crash overheard the whole thing. He wasn't about to let Mandrake's talents go to waste.

"All right," Crash said. "Let's try it this way — give me and the kid five minutes alone with the suspects. If junior doesn't crack the case, you can yank my jacket."

Chief Doyle's lips twisted into a cruel grin. "You're willing to risk your investigator's license on this kid?"

Mandrake gasped.

Crash pinched a strand of lint off his coat. "If the kid doesn't finger the crook in five minutes flat, I'll hightail it out of town, and you'll never see my mug again."

Doyle clapped his hands. "Perfect! Game on! But I'm not leaving you alone."

"Fair enough."

Doyle galloped off to gather the suspects.

Mandrake shuffled over to Crash. "Are you crazy? You could lose your license!"

"Not if you crack the case. You can do this in five minutes, right?"

Amateur Sleuth Rule #3

The Butler didn't do it.

Butlers are gentlefolk. Consider the cook. And don't eat on the job... just in case.

"FIVE MINUTES STARTS NOW." Doyle pressed a button on his watch starting the clock.

Mandrake considered his options. He could run or cry or do both. Solving such a complex mystery was hard enough but doing it in five minutes?! Impossible.

The door swung open and two police officers ushered in the suspects. Leading the way was a blue-power-suited woman with her hair pulled back until her eyelids squeaked. Agatha Highsmith. Mandrake recognized her from the news. She sat on the board of all of the robbed banks. She knew exactly which branches were being staked out tonight and more importantly, which ones were not.

Behind her, a scrawny man with a steel gray crew cut and a security guard uniform.

Mandrake spied the notes Doyle had left on the table. He matched the man's face to the photo of Ambrose Starks. Ambrose was once head of security for the bank chain but had been busted down to night watchman in the wake of the robberies.

Bringing up the rear, wearing a black crushed velvet suit practically vacuum-sealed onto her curvy figure, was recent convict and queen of safe-crackers, Valentine Velvet. Her hair matched her outfit, as did her eyes. And her heart.

"Nice to see you without bars between us, Val," Crash drawled as he leaned against the wall near the door.

"Crash Brickfist." She traced a long finger across his chest. "The one safe I could never open."

"Everybody sit," Doyle barked. "This will only take five minutes." He checked his watch. "Actually, four and a quarter. Better hurry, kid."

Ms. Highsmith sat across from Mandrake. Her eyes squinted at his pajamas."Are those giraffes?"

"I was... uh... undercover," Mandrake sunk a bit in his chair.

"If you don't mind," the security guard, Starks, interrupted, "I'd just as soon get home. I have a TV dinner thawing."

"The kid has a few questions." Crash gave Mandrake a stern look. "Kid..."

"Uh, I... " Mandrake fought to keep his voice from shaking as much as his knees. "Hello suspects! Nice to meet everybody in person and all. This is my first interrogation. Pretty awesome, huh?"

In unison, the group turned toward Doyle. The Chief propped his feet up on the table. "Just play along. It'll all be over very, very soon."

"Ms. Highsmith." A mechanical grinding from a security camera perched high on the wall opposite Mandrake interrupted. Its lens zoomed in on him breaking his train of thought.

"Ahem," Crash growled. "On the clock, kid."

Mandrake shook his head and made a brain-focusing motor-boat sound. "Ms. Highsmith, what's the process for opening the vault downstairs?"

"It's on a time-lock," she sighed. "Scheduled to open tomorrow morning. Any attempt to tamper with it results in the release of acid capsules that fuse the mechanism solid."

"I supervised the installation myself," Starks said. "Absolutely impossible to open at the wrong time."

Valentine smiled. "'Impossible' might be an overstatement."

"Two minutes," Doyle chimed.

Mandrake's heart pounded. He turned to Starks and spoke fast. "Tell me about the security plan for tonight. The police staked out the other banks, which left you in charge of this one?"

Starks glared at Mandrake. "I don't think I like your tone, young sir."

"I'll try to change it." Mandrake said in a high-pitched cartoony girl voice like he was doing a puppet show.

"Normal voice, kid." Crash closed his eyes and rubbed his head in frustration. "Normal voice."

Mandrake focused on Starks, "The police left this bank in your hands, is that right? You were all alone."

"Sure," Starks grumbled. "But nature calls. Especially at my age."

"And you reported these bathroom breaks?"

"Every one of them. As requested by the Chief of Police, himself. I don't shirk my responsibility."

Doyle tapped his watch. "Time's running out. You got one minute."

Crash loosened his collar. "Kid..."

"All good, Crash. I only have one last question." Mandrake's eyes narrowed. "Ms. Velvet, I think we all know you're the only person in the world skilled enough to crack a safe that size."

"You make a girl blush." Valentine fanned herself playfully. "But it's not my bag anymore. I'm all straight and narrow. I was released from the joint early for playing nice."

"Playing nice? Does that mean you made a deal to reduce your prison sentence?"

"All right!" Doyle sprang to his feet. "Time's up, everybody out!"

Crash glanced at his wrist. "Not according to my watch."

"Yeah, well mine's the one that counts. Pack it up, gumshoe. You're done in this town."

Mandrake's gaze held Valentine's. "What did you give to the police to get less time, Ms. Velvet?"

Doyle's face reddened. "I said out!"

Mandrake ignored him. "Or perhaps I should say, what did you give to Chief Doyle?"

A smile stretched across Valentine's slick lips. "I told him my secrets for opening vaults. Gave him a real crash course. Supposedly to prevent further thefts." Valentine stared Doyle in the eyes. "Supposedly."

"Hey kid," Crash chuckled, "exactly when did the Bearded Bandit begin his reign of terror?"

Mandrake checked his phone's calendar. "Just after Ms. Velvet's arrest." Mandrake turned to Chief Doyle. "The first Monday after, to be exact."

"Bowling night," Crash grumbled.

"Two-forty in the seventh frame is impressive bowling, Chief," Mandrake swiveled to Doyle. "Considering three-hundred is a perfect game. You were on a pace for what? Three-thirty."

"How is that possible?" Ms. Highsmith said.

"It's not," Crash cracked his knuckles.

"I guess I miscalculated," Doyle backpedaled from the table. "Those little pencils, you know, they don't have erasers."

"You're thinking of mini-golf, Roger." It was the first time Crash had referred to Doyle by his first name and not 'Chief,' but by this point, everyone in the room realized Doyle was about to be demoted. Including the two cops, who now maneuvered to either side of their boss, watching him.

"The Bandit wears a false beard," Starks interjected. "Doyle already has a beard. Why would he wear a fake?"

"No one would suspect a man who already had a beard and a belly to wear a fake beard and a belly." Mandrake folded his hands before him. "I wonder what we would find if we opened Chief Doyle's bowling bag."

Crash smirked. "I'm betting on a set of fake whiskers."

"And a thin pillow," Mandrake nodded.

Doyle raised his bag, then swung into the two officers, knocking them backwards. He pulled a pistol from the bag and waved it at Crash.

"You don't understand," the Chief cried. "Budget cuts. Chief of Police barely pays the bills in this city. After bringing down the Mimic, I deserved more."

"That money didn't belong to you," Ms. Highsmith said. "You robbed innocent people's bank accounts!"

"This city owes me. I made it pay. I've hidden that money away where no one can get it! Ever! No one can stop me."

Valentine Velvet's lips pulled back further, her smile widening.

Doyle waved the gun at her. "What's so funny, convict?"

"I remember saying that once — 'No one can stop me!'" She slanted her eyes over to Crash. "I was wrong."

Crash stepped forward, clenching his fists. "Kid, it's time. Assume the position."

Mandrake slipped under the table and curled into a tight ball. Ms. Highsmith and Mr. Starks followed his lead.

Not Valentine, though — she sat back and got comfortable. Too bad there wasn't popcorn.

Amateur Sleuth Rule #4a

Stay in school.
There's no money in sleuthing.

Amateur Sleuth Rule 4b:

If you're making money sleuthing, something
is very wrong. You might be a crook. You have
the right to remain silent...

"Inviso postquam schola," screamed the red ink beside the "F" scrawled atop Mandrake's Latin test.

Miss Ellispeters kindly translated: "See me after class."

Unfortunately, the "F" needed no translation.

Master investigator that he was, Mandrake had seen this coming. After his triumphant night at the bank, Mandrake was dumped at school, without books or lunch or sleep or even a chance to change out of his snoring giraffe PJ's.

Worst of all, he was ill prepared for his life-or-death fourth period Latin test.

His stomach hurt. His temples throbbed. And when Grandma found out... shudder.

The red "F" burned his eyes. He flipped the test to the clean failure free blank white canvas.

He fished a pencil from his bag. Drawing always helped him with stress. He could lose himself in the lines and circles and worlds he created. Mandrake was no mindless doodler. He specialized in Forensic art. Like most things law-enforcement-related, Mandrake had a knack for it. A good forensic artist converted eyewitness memories into life-like portraits used to track down crooks.

Despite its technical precision, Mandrake's work had a delicacy, a fineness that had captured the attention of Mr. Gash, his art teacher. Without discussing it with Mandrake, Mr. Gash approached Grandma and arranged for a scholarship at the Argyll Academy of Art. Now, Grandma planned to ship him away from Capital City to this new art school in a tiny town called Poodle Springs. Poodle Springs, whose major crimes involved the theft of pies cooling on windowsills and brazen lemonade stand heists.

On the page, a thick mustache appeared, then a face. A monocle clenched in its left eye. A square jaw. A slightly cocked hunter's cap topped it off. All of this framed by the turned-up collar of a London Fog jacket.

It was a sketch of the greatest detective to ever live, Inspector Gunther Gates.

This rendition was from the Inspector's younger days when he was splashed across the cover of every national magazine and featured on every TV show, championing the celebrity crime-stopper's capture of Capital City's most notorious villains — Max and Mindy Mandrake. The villains otherwise known as Mandrake's parents.

Miss Ellispeters' incomprehensible drone suddenly snapped silent. A pair of men hovered just outside the classroom door. Miss Ellispeters went to them.

The visitors appeared identical, in their boyish faces and hairstyles, and in their clothing. They wore curiously indistinguishable suits with short, belted jackets and pants that ended just below their knees. From there down were brightly colored socks and brown-and-white saddle-style shoes. They might have been golfers. Colorblind golfers.

Their matching bow ties and socks came in contrasting colors: blue for the man on the right, red on the left.

Miss Ellispeters and the men exchanged hushed whispers and for a moment Mandrake's teacher's face grew red. She shook her head angrily.

And then in unison, the three of them turned and stared directly at Mandrake.

He waved and they looked away.

The school bell blared. Students packed up their things and streamed out of the classroom. In the chaotic scramble, Mandrake lost sight of the strange twins.

He thought about hiding in the crowd to evade his teacher's wrath, but he'd just have to face her again tomorrow. Might as well get it over with. He approached her desk, test in hand. "You wanted to see me, Miss Ellispeters?"

She snatched the paper from his hand, pulled out her red pen and crossed out the "F" and replaced it with a "D".

"We were unaware," she muttered, "of extenuating circumstance."

Then, after an additional moment of thought, scribbled a plus sign, upgrading Mandrake to a D plus.

Mandrake gazed at the new grade. He hadn't mentioned his run-in with the Bearded Bank Bandit to her, or anyone.

"We shall be expecting better of you in the future, young man," Miss Ellispeters wiggled her penciled in eyebrows. "We are led to believe you will be undergoing tutelage."

"We are?" Mandrake hadn't heard anything more about tutoring since Crash mentioned it to his grandmother the night before last.

She politely smiled and returned her attention to a stack of homework. "Off you go."

Mandrake nodded, put his head down and shuffled away. His face smashed into a coffee stained tie. The neckwear was attached to every student of Gunther Gates Middle School's worst nightmare — Vice Principal Lestrade.

"Mandrake."

The boy's name being what it was, he couldn't be sure, but the way Lestrade said it, it felt like a last name.

"My office. NOW."

Amateur Sleuth Rule #5

Be suspicious of people who insist on doing it 'by the book'. I've never seen this book. No one has. Which makes them liars, or delusional.

"I DON'T KNOW WHAT YOU'RE UP TO, BOY. But I will find out," Lestrade said playing, this whole thing like a rookie detective trying to sweat out a perp.

Mandrake sat in the hot-seat across from his sinister Vice Principal. The chair was purposefully hard and stiff-backed, part of the psychological warfare Lestrade waged. He preferred to keep students uncomfortable in his presence. He needn't have bothered; no piece of furniture could ever compete with the deep dread cast by his dark demeanor and even darker reputation.

Lestrade wasn't a long man, more square-ish, almost as wide as he was tall. But he gave the impression of being big, keeping his shoulders hunched forward at all times, his round belly hard like he was smuggling cannonballs beneath the short sleeve shirts he wore under his suit jacket.

Mandrake was willing to bet the tie clipped on.

"This comes from the top." Lestrade slid a crisp sealed envelope across the desk to Mandrake. "I don't like when people go over my head. I don't like it at all."

Mandrake sheepishly took the envelope.

"Now get back to class." Lestrade said, swiveling in his chair to a bank of security monitors which spied on the school hallways.

Mandrake slinked out of the office and hurried down the hall. As he rounded the corner, he dug a finger under the seal of the envelope and ripped it open.

Inside, he fished out a folded letter. He straightened it and read its simple message:

"Baker St. Library, 4pm, M-W-F. For Latin instruction."

Something smelled.

Something smelled... lemony.

Mandrake pressed his nostrils in the center of the paper and took a deep whiff of the fresh citric scent. It came from fruit and not a cleaning product or perfume.

Mandrake tucked the letter away.

He knew the solution to this sour-scented mystery lay at the steps of the Baker Street Library, and hopefully had nothing to do with Latin.

Amateur Sleuth Rule #6

Always poke a wall portrait between the eyes, just in case.

Grandma steered her ancient sedan to the curb of The Baker Street Library. From the cracked granite steps, an old fellow with the crooked briar pipe and priest collar rose to greet them.

Grandma rolled down the window and the man strode to the car and lifted his hat, revealing a wisp of unkempt hair that stuck up from the front of his otherwise hairless head like an exotic white hothouse flower.

"Good afternoon, madam," he said, his voice a brogue that sounded like all of Ireland had been distilled into his vocal chords. "I'm Father Seamus."

Mandrake slid out on the passenger side, as Father continued, "I'll be responsible for the boy's instruction in Latin every Monday, Wednesday, and Friday. He'll be finished with his lessons and at the curb promptly at eight sharp."

"Eight sharp?" Grandma said. "A little late for a school night?"

"He shan't be out pitching pennies and rolling barrel-hoops, I assure you." Father Seamus gave her a wide grin. "His time will be well-spent."

Grandma stared up at the ancient and dilapidated building behind her. "I thought they shut this place down, after the incident."

Mandrake's ears perked. Incident?

"It's still open... to members. Not to the public," Seamus said.

Grandma narrowed her eyes in a gaze Mandrake new quite well. "I expect to see results."

"So do we," Seamus countered.

The round-faced priest hummed an old Irish tune as they watched Grandma drive off. Behind them, the Baker Street Library loomed like a fortress of drab brick, with its steel bars over the windows and the two imposing stone dogs guarding either side of the wide steps out front.

Seamus laid a hand on the boy's shoulder. "Well, lad, are you ready for adventure?"

"Adventure?" Mandrake questioned. "Latin is literally the opposite of adventure."

Father Seamus grinned and led the way up the stone steps to the library doors. Mandrake followed, studying the canine statues guarding over the staircase. "Bloodhounds, right?"

"Noble creatures," Seamus responded as he stopped at the colossal wooden doors. "Their highly-tuned sense of smell has aided man in search and detection for centuries."

The priest reached into his pocket and pulled out a single laminated library card.

"Members only." Seamus swiped the card through a small black card reader attached to the door frame.

A loud thud deep inside the aged wood heralded the disengagement of the massive lock.

Seamus reached for the huge round knob and the door's oiled hinges glided easily, soundlessly. "After you."

Amateur Sleuth Rule #7

When looking for secret passages, be careful not to twist fixtures so hard you cause permanent damage.

"Come along, young lad," Seamus's lilting Irish tenor sang from the darkness. "Tempus fugit! Time flies!"

Mandrake shuffled ahead. His vision wrestled with the gloom. In the marble floor beneath his feet, he spied the reflection of a high ceiling and the hanging light fixture with bulbs that flickered like candle-flames. A few sconces trickled scant light, revealing plank walls and rich but dusty tapestries. Further, through an arch, they moved through ranks and ranks of bookshelves, filled to the rafters with dust-coated, leather-bound volumes.

Mandrake wondered if this place even had a paperback book, much less free Wi-Fi.

Seamus's pipe smoke curled and snaked in the slatted sunlight that knifed through the venetian blinds. "So, tell me what you know, young Mandrake."

"About Latin?" Mandrake shrugged. "Not much."

Father Seamus chuckled, barely audible. "So then, what about other things? Your exploits with Mr. Brickfist, for example?"

Mandrake squirmed. "I'm not sure what you're talking about."

"Oh? I expect our disgraced police chief knows exactly what I'm talking about. As does the Electric Pineapple Mob. And the Mimic. And Dr. Notorious. And Jimmy 'the Elbow' Macaroni. And Moxie Mallory and her All-Girl Gang."

"That's Moxie Malloy. No 'r'," Mandrake interrupted. "Not that

I'd know anything about that." Mandrake cast his eyes around the room looking for clues to Seamus's real motives. "Why am I really here?"

"Ah, what fun is a mystery, if there's nothing mysterious about it?" Father Seamus quickened his step as if he had somewhere to be. "And all you need is The Nose to figure it out."

Seamus was way ahead of Mandrake, who hardly noticed, too busy examining the brown stains in the ceiling, and spying the mammoth and archaic wooden Card Catalogue in the center of it all.

"Why did this library close down?" Mandrake chased Seamus around the corner into a small cul-de-sac of books.

But.

Seamus was gone.

Vanished.

Like a magician.

Mandrake faced a wall of books and two additional towering shelves on either side. A dead end. The bookcases stretched to the ceiling. There was nowhere for Seamus to duck or hide. It was as if Seamus had just evaporated in a puff of smoke or ghost-walked through the bookshelf.

A whistle came, in the distance. That old Irish tune. But with the strange acoustics of the old building it was impossible to tell where.

Excitement rippled through Mandrake's bones. There was a mystery to solve and it had nothing to do with Latin. Mandrake wanted to high-five himself, but decided against it. Someone might be watching, after all. And he wasn't confident of the mechanics of a selfie high-five. Stick to mysteries, Sleuth-boy.

Opposite the dead-end of books, against the far wall, a few comfy-looking reading chairs surrounded a table. There, books propped on stands, each open to various pages, all of them thick and bound in the finest leather.

A bronze bust of an eagle-nosed human head sat at the center of all this. Hollow eyes, prominent brows, sunken cheeks.

Sherlock Holmes.

Hmmm... A curious choice. Ironic, even. Or suspicious.

The shelved books sported a small white label with numbers. The Dewey Decimal System. Mandrake rubbed his baby-soft chin. The books in this section were labeled with a "364" to the left of the decimal. Mandrake browsed the titles — Criminology Handbook, Readings in Criminology, Criminology for Dummies, Criminology and Punishology.

Mandrake sighed. He had little use for books about crime-solving. He had The Nose.

The Nose?! Of course! He grabbed the very letter that brought him here from his inside jacket pocket and gave it a sniff.

Ahhh. Lemons!

Mandrake raced over to one of the large lamps that sat by the reading table and removed its shade. With two hands he spread the citrus-smelling invitation wide and held it just above the glowing naked light bulb. The note appeared ordinary enough, hand written ink on mundane unlined paper. The only thing remarkable about it was its bitter stench, and while scented stationary remained a remote possibility, Mandrake suspected something far more intriguing.

The bulb warmed the paper. A previously invisible writing materialized on the untouched backside of the note. It was an old spy trick. Any acidic liquid could be use to send an invisible ink message — onion juice, vinegar, oranges, and, of course, lemons. Within moments the full juice-scrawled message became legible:

"Find the RED SCOOTER. Love, Annie Alexis Graham"

Mandrake returned back to the wall of Criminology hardbacks and paced. What did RED SCOOTER have to do with Criminology? Perhaps it was a book title? Or an author's name? Or an infamous getaway car used in a ridiculously juvenile bank heist?

Too simple. Too obvious. Too dumb.

He went back to the invisible ink and looked for more clues.

What about "Annie Alexis Graham"? He recognized something in the name, but he couldn't quite say what.

This called for a web search! He pulled out his cell phone.

"No Connection," the phone displayed.

Mandrake needed information. Where was he going to get it?

Books. He was in a library. Duh.

He hurried to the huge set of wooden drawers, each with a small paper tab under a black metal pull.

The Card Catalogue.

Annie Alexis Graham was likely an author, not a title. He slid open the cabinet labeled "GR-GU" — for the last name, Graham, and stared at the long line of thousands of cards. He sped through them in chunks, skipping past titles and subjects and authors—

His fingers slowed, then stopped at a card with a single author — "GRAHAM, ARTHUR P." Too far. He reversed course and retreated through Graham after Graham — GRAHAM, ANGIE, GRAHAM, ANDREW, GRAHAM ANDERS.

Annie Graham wasn't among them, nor was Annie Alexis Graham or A Graham or Anne A Graham —

Wait.

Anne A Graham.

Of course! That was it! It wasn't a name, it was a clue!

An anagram! A word or phrase that could be made by scrambling the letters of another word.

Mandrake hurried back to the criminology section.

Whirrrrrrrr. The noise froze Mandrake. His ears perked. Normally, such a soft sound would go undetected, but in the pin-drop silence of the library it roared like a firecracker to Mandrake's razor sharp senses.

His eyes drifted to the mysterious letter. He pretended to focus on solving its riddles and took another large step.

Whirrrrrrrr.

The sound was coming from the bust of Sherlock Holmes. Mandrake took another few steps. The sound came again. He had detected the very same grinding in the Capital City Bank offices the night he brought down the Bearded Bank Bandit: the sound of a camera lens adjusting its zoom.

Someone was watching!

Who? Crash Brickfist? Seamus? A psychotic librarian?

Mandrake peeled off his coat and pretended to search for a place to hang it. "Hello? Father Seamus?" He called out, not expecting an answer. "Is there a coat-rack around?" He shuffled toward the bust. "This is my school coat. A Christmas present. I can't just put it on this dirty floor. Hello?"

Again, no response.

"Okaaaay then, I'll just... " Mandrake stared the bronze Sherlock right in the nostrils. There, a small drilled hole right in Sherlock's long nose, the perfect place to stick a spy camera. "...improvise."

Mandrake tossed his jacket over the head of the statue completely covering its face. "Problem solved."

His privacy restored, Mandrake pulled out his phone and flipped it to camera mode. He perched the phone on top of his coat where the brim of Sherlock's deerstalker hat jutted out and aimed it at the dead-end of bookcases, trying to replicate the hidden camera's view. His fingers worked the zoom, guesstimating the default frame of the average spy-cam. Once satisfied, he hit record, and stepped back into the center of the Criminology section, returning his attention to the letter and its lemonicous anagram.

"Red Scooter." Mandrake visualized the letters on wooden tiles. He began to mentally shuffle them — RED SCOOTER became CRED

ROOSTER then CRED ROOSTER became CODE ROSTER which then became CODE SORTER.

Hmmm. 'CODE' could mean many things. The inner-workings of a computer program perhaps or maybe text hidden in plain sight like the anagram itself. But SORTER didn't really fit here. Mandrake moved on.

CORD STEREO -RECORDS TOE - RED COOTERS —

Mandrake rubbed his temples. He wanted to quit but he knew finding meaningful patterns held the secret —

Wait. The secret. The SECRET! He rearranged the tiles in his brain space.

SECRET

But Secret what?

"Secret... Odor!" he punched the air in celebration. Then slumped. Uh, no way. Come on, "Secret Odor"? Reaaaally?

Mandrake shook his head. Back to mind-puzzles:

"S-E-C-R-E-T-O-D-O-R"

His brain slid the "D" one letter to the left, swapping it with the "O".

"S-E-C-R-E-T-D-O-O-R" That's it!

He raced back to the Criminology books. The game had shifted. Typically, secret doors could be opened by pushing or pulling the right book or combination of books from amongst the shelves. A lesser detective might try to brute-force their way to a solution by randomly pulling books, hoping to stumble upon the triggering tome. Mandrake scorned such clumsy solutions. What if pulling the wrong book triggered a lock or an alarm or a booby-trap? Better to choose wisely. Mandrake's eyes scanned the shelves. Anything could be a clue. Book bindings, titles, placement or groupings.

Mandrake's eyes narrowed. A grin twisted at the corner of his mouth.

"THE INSPECTOR SPEAKS by Inspector Gunther Gates," he read from the binding of the book that sat just off center in the book shelf on the right.

A surge of adrenaline warmed him. He knew the book. He'd never read it. Grandma forbid it. It seemed too much of a coincidence that the clues all led to a memoir created by Mandrake's esteemed sleuthing spirit animal.

He slid the book off the shelf. Clack! It caught on something, as if it was on a track that had reached its limit.

There was nothing else. No sound of gears or tumbling locks or whoosh of air.

Bummer.

Time to give up. He turned to yell out to Father Seamus. The floor had vanished in front of him. His feet poked over the edge of a wide opening... a dark pit. Inside, just beneath him, stretched a winding stone staircase.

He carefully tip-toed down the rocky steps. "Hello?" His voice echoed off the stone walls and around the seemingly endless circle of stairs.

No answer came. Perhaps it wasn't smart to continue down this

—

BAM! The entrance above him slid back in place, trapping him inside.

Father Seamus's words suddenly reverberated in Mandrake's mind — "Well, lad, are you ready for adventure?"

AMATEUR SLEUTH RULE #8:

Spiral staircases never lead to anything good.

AFTER THREE HUNDRED AND SEVENTY-SIX jagged stone steps of death, the sinister stairway emptied into a dungeon-like chamber of stone floors and dripping rock. From the curved architecture, Mandrake guessed it was once a subway tunnel.

While tracks and trains had long gone, this place was far from defunct. Its walls were furnished with racks of weaponry, ranging from axes and guillotines to long test-tubes filled with brightly colored toxins. One section of the room displayed tanks filled with piranhas, cobras, and big hairy tarantulas. In another section stood a gang of curiously dressed and faceless mannequins.

Mandrake read a plaque at the foot of one dressed in an elegant tuxedo and top hat — Don Romeo Amador, the Lady-killer. Beside it, "Terror" Annie Bonnett, Frontier Murderess, the mannequin displaying a blocky imitation of a woman wearing a gingham dress with white frills at the hems, a massive cleaver in its hand.

He shifted his eyes to the next tableau, a male and female pair. The male figure was slight, in drab, nondescript clothes, hair that stuck up in a few places, not unlike Mandrake's own messy mop-top, but otherwise no distinguishing characteristics whatsoever. And just slightly behind that one, the female figure, this one tall and athletic-looking, dressed for action in a dark leather jumpsuit bristling with weapons.

These didn't have identifying plaques. And yet, there was something... familiar.

And then one of them spoke. "Whyncha take a picture, kid? It'll last longer."

Mandrake jumped back and struck a feeble karate pose, ready to do battle with this possessed dummy.

Behind the mannequins, leaning against a heavy set of sliding doors, was Crash Brickfist. "Shake a leg kid. These crimes that ain't gonna solve themselves."

Crash pushed the doors open and led Mandrake into a large conference room. An oddball group sat around a long wooden table, their attention absorbed by a large bank of video monitors suspended at the far end of the room.

They didn't notice Mandrake slip in behind them.

The large screens showed Mandrake pacing in the Criminology section. Mandrake chuckled. His trick had worked perfectly. The assembled group assumed it was a live feed. He'd created a video with his phone and perched the screen in front of the Sherlock bust's spying eyes.

"I thought you said this kid had The Nose," said a penny-brown-haired teenage girl in a demure pleated plaid jumper. She lifted a dainty wrist and checked her watch. "He hasn't even figured out the anagram yet."

Around the room other videos played out — Mandrake interrogating the suspects at the Capital City bank, Mandrake practicing Aikido on a row of stuff animals in his bedroom, Mandrake failing to climb the rope in gym class.

"This is a catastrophe," cried a French-accented voice from the round little man at far end of the table. He stroked his tidily-waxed mustache with one hand as he raised his half-empty glass with his other. "I'm going to need more wine."

"Give him a chance, Achille," Father Seamus watched the action through pipe smoke. "We need this."

Need this? Mandrake's heart jumped. He held back squealing. "This" meaning… him?

"Father Seamus is right," two men said in unison. Mandrake recognized them as the ones who had interrupted Miss Ellispeters' Latin class. They still wore the same curious matching suits and caps, bow ties in contrasting colors. "The clues were unusually challenging."

"Not that challenging," Mandrake strode forward.

The group turned. Flabbergasted.

"But you're up there," one of the bow tie-wearing men protested while pointing dumbly at the monitor.

"He was up there," the Asian man stroked his whiskers.

"A recorded video," the Frenchman toasted him.

"Likely made when he draped the coat over the bust," the teeny-bopper girl said.

"And carefully placed in front of our security cameras on a stack of books," the red bow-tied man said.

"Harrumph," the girl harrumphed.

"But how on earth were you able to figure out the mathematical puzzle so quickly?" the blue bow-tied man asked.

"Well... uh... ," Mandrake uttered in confusion. He didn't figure out any math. He hated math more than Latin. He decided to keep that little nugget to himself.

"Beginner's luck, perhaps?" Seamus flipped the main TV to cartoons.

"Impossible," the Asian man stroked his chin beard. "There are currently thirty-six-thousand-three-hundred and nine shelved books in the Baker Street library. The boy had a one in thirty-six-thousand-three-hundred and nine chance of guessing right."

"Then, I'd say there's a one hundred percent chance he cheated." The girl crossed her arms. "He looks like a cheater."

"The kid's not a cheat," Crash interrupted.

The blue bow-tied man stopped pacing. "Are you suggesting he was able to tally all of the books in the entire Baker Street Library and realize that number — 36,309 — corresponded to the only book in the Dewey Decimal system with that number — AN INSPECTOR SPEAKS — Code — 363.09 — all in twenty-three minutes?"

The Asian Man furrowed his brow. "A tally of that many books in that amount of time could not be made by the average human mind. It would take a mathematical genius or some kind of numerical savant or —"

"Dust." Mandrake raised a dirty index finger.

"Dust, of course!" Red bow-tie exclaimed. Then wrinkled his face in confusion. "Huh?"

Mandrake grinned. "This library hasn't been used in years. All the books on the shelves have a thick layer of dust. But since Father Seamus and the rest of you had to touch a specific book to gain entry into this chamber... It was simply a matter of identifying the one book that wasn't caked in decades of dust."

The faces around the table froze. He had rendered the room completely speechless.

"Told ya we need a maid," the girl commented.

"Maybe it's time we let the kid in on why he's here," Crash urged.

"And whom he addresses," the Frenchman raised a perfumed handkerchief to his lips.

"Mandrake Mandrake," announced the girl in the jumper, "you've just stumbled into the headquarters of The Secret Society of the Sleuthing Seven."

"The Sleuthing Seven, for short," the Frenchman clarified.

"The Seven, for shorter," Crash Brickfist said.

"Well... uh...," Mandrake shuffled. "Cool?"

The group responded with narrowed looks and tense squints. Apparently, a bigger reaction was called for.

Father Seamus cut through the tension. "The Seven is a league of the world's finest detectives."

The Frenchman nodded. "We solve the crimes the authorities cannot."

"The Society has been cracking the un-crackable for years." Crash cracked his knuckles. Mandrake guessed it wasn't ironic. Crash wasn't much of a pun-guy.

"The Society has been around for hundreds of years, actually," one of the twins added.

"I think you're ready to be a part of it," Crash laid a heavy hand on Mandrake's shoulder.

"Perhaps it goes without saying, but Monsieur Brickfist does not speak for the entire organization." The Frenchman sniffed at his wine. "We are unsure you have what it takes."

Mandrake's face went flush. He was sick of being judged. Hadn't he shown them enough by solving their silly riddles? By bringing down the Bearded Bank Bandit? By Ninja punching his favorite Teddy Bear? It was time to turn the tables. He appraised them over the rims of his glasses. "And how am I so sure... you have what it takes?"

This comment drew some "did someone step in dog poop" looks around the table.

"If this club is so awesome sauce," Mandrake asked, with a touch of resentment, "how come I've never heard of it?"

"We're so awesome sauce, no one's ever heard of us." The teenage girl tapped her expensive shoes in annoyance.

Mandrake scowled. "I've never heard of a secret fraternity of aardvark jockeys, either, but that doesn't mean I'm impressed by the idea."

This brought more confusion from the assembled. One of the bowties went scrambling through his papers actually searching for research on aardvarks.

"It just seems unfair — why am I the one having to prove

anything? You couldn't even figure out the camera trick I pulled or the dust thing —"

The collective sleuths stammered for answers.

Mandrake continued. "From what I see, you're not qualified to judge me. I don't even know who you people are!"

The Frenchman slammed his wine down. "What an arrogant little pestilence is this one! I am inclined to cast my vote already."

The Asian man folded his hands. "Now, now, the young man has a point. How can we ask him to be forthcoming without being such ourselves?" He stood and bowed very slightly. "I am Lung."

"Lung? Like Professor Lung?" Mandrake eyes widened. "The legendary Professor Lung who brought down the Ring of Nine? The Professor Lung who solved the Mystery of Macabre Manor and single-handily defeated Mao-Tan the Master? That Professor Lung?"

Lung bowed in reply. "At your service."

"But... you must be over a hundred years old!"

"In the immortal words of Sun Tzu — none of your stinking business."

"My acquaintance, you've already made," said Father Seamus. "But perhaps you aren't aware of my history. Modesty prevents excess detail, but you've heard of the Maltese Madonna?"

"The statue stolen from the Vatican gallery?" Mandrake's jaw dropped. "That was you?"

"Not the theft! The recovery! "Father Seamus signed the cross. "I'm a holy man. I have commandments."

"I'm Abbey Prue," the snarky girl said in a polished diction that reflected an expensive education. "Not that I have to prove anything to you, but I'm the one who took down the Alexiev counterfeit ring."

"The one in October Falls? I followed that case!" Mandrake searched his memory. "But I never heard about you. That was broken by a small-town sheriff named —"

"Sheriff Abner Prue," she finished. "Daddy took all the credit."

Mandrake sighed. He knew a thing or two about adults stealing credit for the good deeds of kids.

Abbey waved a hand as if to erase her last comment. "But I'm flying solo now. Making my own path. I've been rocking this whole Secret Seven gig for about a year now."

"Ooh, ooh, next!" The bow-tied men waved their hands wildly. "We're the Farley Boys, Frankie and Freddy." They pointed at each other by way of introduction.

"Like in the books?" Mandrake asked.

"Not like the books." Frankie shook his head emphatically. He was the one with the red tie. "From the books! They were based on our true-life boyhood adventures."

"But you're not exactly boys," Mandrake said. "You're wearing toupees."

"We still have boyish charm." Freddy adjusted his hairpiece. "We were teenage sleuths, much like yourself."

"We've been in the Society since Inspector Gates brought us onboard," Frankie said. "He mentored us, really."

"Inspector Gates?!" Mandrake squealed. "Is he part of this?"

"Uck. A fanboy." Abbey rolled her eyes.

"Inspector Gates is the face of the team," O'Malley said. "The Detective-in-Chief."

"Is he here? Now?" Mandrake looked around. "Can I get a selfie? Do you think he'd sign my magnifying glass?"

The detectives exchanged curious glances, unsure of how to respond.

"Let's keep going with the intros," Crash grumbled. "Frenchie, you're next."

"Moi? Of course," said the Frenchman at the end of the table. "I am, naturellement, Monsieur Achille Pinot."

He waited for Mandrake's reaction, but the boy just stared at him blankly.

"The famed consulting detective?"

Mandrake shrugged.

"Inspecteur général of the police nationale, retired? Surely you have heard of me!"

Mandrake shook his head. Nope. Never.

"N'en faire pas, never to mind. I am the current custodian of this assembly, and as such it is my responsibility to ensure that the roster is made up of the finest investigative minds in the world." He stared at Mandrake, all of the trappings of foppish vanity gone, replaced by a look of steely inquisition. "Are you one of these minds, Monsieur Mandrake?"

Mandrake fumbled, "I... um... "

"The kid's the real deal," Crash said.

"We can't just let this baby in!" Abbey Prue slammed a fist on the table. "We have standards! This is ridiculous."

"Ridiculous times call for ridiculous measures," Father Seamus said.

"I'd put my sleuthing skills up against any of you," Mandrake said. "I've cracked a lot of cases. It's just someone else always gets the credit."

"Your sleuthing skills aren't in question," Freddy Farley said. "In fact, it's long been theorized that detective abilities might be at their peak between the ages of ten and thirteen."

"Really?" Mandrake beamed.

"Because kids are too dumb to know what's impossible," Abbey said. "It's your lack of limits that makes you special —"

"And dangereux," Pinot chimed.

"The age requirement is in place for reasons of safety. Sleuthing is a dangerous business," Freddy Farley said.

"There must be someone with more experience," Lung said. "Someone with a college degree or some sort of online certificate in sleuthing."

"You want to try another finger-print and DNA type?" Crash huffed. "I'd rather someone with street smarts than some Harvard know-it-all coming in here throwing ten dollar words around."

"Our research hasn't uncovered a single adult fitting our criteria." Freddy Farley began sifting through a nearly four-foot-high tower of file folders precariously balanced on the tables.

His brother Frankie picked up the thought, "Once a kid with the proper aptitude gets into high-school their imaginations and ability to conjure up solutions to complex mysteries gets flushed down the toilet. They become more interested in videogames, and sports and girls."

"Sometimes boys," Abbey added.

Freddy Farley searched through the files. "We haven't seen a detective old enough to shave on our radar since all those CSI TV shows got so popular. Now all the crime-fighters want to be chemists."

"Chemists!" Pinot exclaimed "Sacre Bleu! Television is killing our youth!"

"There's a mystery-solving dog in Toledo," Freddy said.

"I'm allergic to dogs," Father O'Malley said, stuffing an éclair in his mouth.

"I'm not picking up no poop," Crash added.

"Well then," Pinot tucked his reading glasses away. "Mr. Brickfist, if you would like to officially state your nomination."

Crash kept it short, "I nominate the kid."

"Before we vote, does anyone at the table have a reason Mr. Mandrake shouldn't be nominated?" Pinot turned up his palms in invitation.

Frank Farley raised his hand and waved it to get attention.

"Just say it," Pinot ordered.

"Well... like I said in my notes... I've impartially surveyed the members of the Seven and each of us is terrified that if the boy even has a fraction of his parent's inclinations —"

Mandrake slammed the table with his hands. "I'm not my parents!"

Everyone stared at him, worried what he might do next.

Mandrake softened his voice to avoid seeming too "master-villain." "I've never even met them. They left me alone on some bridge when I was a baby. The only thing they ever gave me was my stupid name and a lot of super-villain baggage! Try making friends when your parents were once Public Enemy Number 1! And now this? You're scared of me? I thought you were supposed to be some great crime-fighting crew. I'm just a kid. You should all be embarrassed." He pointed at all of them judgmentally. "Shame!"

"Duly noted," Pinot huffed. "We'll go around ze table. Monsieur Crash?"

Crash shrugged. "You know my vote. The kid stays."

Pinot tallied the vote on a piece of paper, "Madame Abbey?"

"Against," she said. "But not because I'm scared. He's just a stupid little boy. What's to be scared of? Other than boogers and cooties and B.O."

Mandrake secretly sniffed his arm pits. Another layer of deodorant wouldn't hurt.

Pinot continued, "Farley Boys?"

"Against," They both said at once.

"I was kind of hoping for the dog," Freddy Farley said.

Pinot scratched two more votes in the no column. "And Professor Lung?"

Lung stared down at Mandrake, appraising him like a jeweler trying to figure out if he was real or counterfeit. "Against."

Pinot took note. "That's quatre against and un for. Father O'Malley?"

O'Malley sighed. "I'm sorry my boy. Against."

"And I am also voting against. The vote is fini." With that Pinot looked up. "Thank you for coming, Monsieur Mandrake."

The detectives burst into side-chatter. Talking about Mandrake, and age restrictions, and sleuthing dogs, as if Mandrake wasn't even in the room.

Crash rested a heavy hand on Mandrake's shoulder and ushered the boy away.

Mandrake's face reddened with anger. "It's not fair! I brought down the Bearded Bank Bandit! You know what I can do! All those cases that Chief Doyle got the glory for! He got promoted to Chief because of what I did. And I can't even get into your stupid detective club!"

"Easy, kid." Crash escorted Mandrake outside the door. "Give me a sec."

He eased the door shut. Mandrake pressed his ear to the old wood. He heard murmuring, hushed voices. He caught pieces of the conversation — "The boy's father!" and "Imminent danger!" and "Given the current threat!"

Then there was silence. Mandrake pushed his head tight against the frame.

The doors burst open.

Once again, Crash loomed over him. He whipped out a solid gold library card. "Welcome to the club, kid."

Mandrake gasped. He'd never won anything or been invited to a club. His amazing feats of detectivity had always been overlooked. This was real validation! He took it and squealed and did a little touchdown dance.

Crash frowned. "Don't do that."

Mandrake stopped right in the middle of the funky-chicken. "Sorry, got carried away."

"It's important to maintain your cover, even with your Grandmother. If she finds out, this done."

Grandma. How could he keep this big a secret? He'd never hidden anything from her before.

Crash looked him in the eyes. "I know you don't want to lie to your grandma, but if we keep getting you home and you bring your grades up, she won't have any reason to suspect anything."

Mandrake checked the time on his phone — 8:05pm. "I'm late. I'd better hurry."

"You know the way out?"

Mandrake nodded and stepped toward the spiral staircase, then stopped. "Oh... seven... but there's eight of us, right? With the Inspector —"

"Oh, I guess you didn't get that part," Crash said with grumbley gravitas. "The Inspector's gone missing. We're hoping you can help us find him."

Amateur Sleuth Rule #9

Dead men don't wear pajamas.

That night, Mandrake decided to read himself to sleep. He slid on his sheep-print pajamas, flipped off his bedside lamp, and snapped on his web-purchased Russian military surplus night-vision goggles.

Tonight he was going to read a forbidden book.

On his way out of the library, Mandrake snagged the leather bound copy of "The Inspector Speaks: A Memoir of the Man Who Brought Down the Mandrakes" from the dusty Criminology shelves and stashed it into his backpack.

It was a library after all. He was just borrowing.

Mandrake scanned the table of contents. His reading violated the negotiated terms of 'The Talk'.

The Talk occurred two years ago, one late summer night, while Grandma hemmed Mandrake's 'school pants', a bi-annual humiliation. Her dentured mouth armed with sewing needles, Grandma suddenly grew ashen, put down her measuring tape, and stared him right in his eyes. "You know, if you have any questions about your Mom, you need to come to me. No one else. Okay? Just me. There are a lot of lies out there. I'll set you straight."

Mandrake nodded and swore, only her. But he had his fingers crossed. So legally he was in the clear. It wasn't that he didn't trust her. He did. One-hundred percent. But Grandma's little girl had once been on the most wanted list. She married the most feared man in the world. She died tragically on a bridge. While all this was back-story to Mandrake, Grandma still felt the pain. She flipped the channel when ace news-caster, Giles Geronimo, mentioned the anniversary of Max's arrest. She faked 'allergies' the time Capital City Magazine listed her little girl as number four on their Most Evil Ever list. Grandma had carefully embargoed Mandrake from any news about his parents.

It left Mandrake in a difficult spot. He knew less about his parents than most of the denizens of Capital City. Now that he was part of the Secret Seven, he needed to come up to speed. Fast. But not through Grandma. He couldn't tell her about his new top secret library card. But he also refused to force her back down that tortured road of painful memories.

Guilt simmered in him, as he opened the forbidden book to page one:

"This book is dedicated to myself."

He sighed. Only eight-hundred-and-seventy-five pages to go. He flipped ahead. A dense world of words stared back at him, not a picture or funny illustration in sight. Mandrake groaned. Why couldn't the Inspector have written a Graphic Novel?

The boy skipped pages at a time, then chapters scanning words as they flew by.

The early sections were focuses on the Inspector's prodigy-like childhood, his potty-training, and his pet llama. He devoted an entire chapter to his middle name. Later chapters seemed to focus on name dropping — his post-fame friendships with Hollywood ingénues and a mother-lode of photos and descriptions about his burgeoning art career. He skipped past chapters on the Inspector's signature silver timepiece (Sally, yes, he named it), how he ironed his shirts, and even a secret family recipe for Amish potato salad.

Then he flipped to Chapter 12 and gasped.

The title alone made his heart skip a beat:

"CHAPTER 12: HOW I BROUGHT DOWN THE MANDRAKES!"

Mandrake's eyes lingered on the words, not daring to drift lower. Curiosity burned inside of him. But what if Grandma knew what she was doing. What if he needed her protection? What if there was something buried in his parents' infamous past that would hurt him in ways he could never heal from?

Whiiiiiiir. A soft mechanical grinding tingled his ears. He might not have noticed it over the low hum of the central heat, except the noise was all too familiar. He'd heard it in Capitol City and then again when the secret camera tracked him in the Criminology section of the library.

Someone had planted a camera in his room.

Mandrake's mind raced. It must be the Seven. He'd seen the video screens displaying all the secret recordings of him. Videos of his most private moments.

But now? Still? He was a member of their group. He was in fact the Seventh. Did they still not trust him? Was this a safety net in case he went all 'Max Mandrake' and decided to terrorize the city? They didn't want him in the group, maybe when he got angry, they decided he needed to be observed like some wounded animal.

Mandrake growled behind the cover of the open book. How rude! How dare they sneak a spy-camera into his sacred kid-cave? His own personal fortress of tween-a-tude. The very place he sometimes liked to cuddle up with a stuffed penguin or two, or slip into superhero jammies or shred the neck of his air-guitar while lip-syncing to mp3s.

He slammed the book shut.

This. Was. Unacceptable.

He narrowed his night-vision gaze on a ridiculous overstuffed pink-polka-dot elephant.

Mr. Peanuts.

Grandma had won the stuffed animal at the Firehouse Carnival Night last fall. Mandrake didn't like elephants, especially pink ones, and the polka-dots didn't help. That's why the prize had been exiled to the inflatable chair in the far corner of Mandrake's room.

The perfect place for its glassy eyes to keep watch on his entire room.

Mandrake hopped to his feet. He didn't bother with his slippers. He meant business. Slipper-less business. He stuck his face all up in Mr. P's personal space. Eye to Night-Vis. Nose to trunk.

"I know what you're doing." Mandrake poked its fluffy chest. "Your little game is up."

Mr. Peanuts stared back, poker-faced, forever locked in that doofy smile.

"I'm a card carrying member of The Secret Society of the Sleuthing Seven," Mandrake poked his pink plushy chest. "I have a right to my privacy!"

Mandrake stared deep into Mr. Peanuts' plastic gaze, searching for the camera within. "I'm done with your stupid tests! I can help you, we both know that. But only if you're straight with me."

Mandrake lifted Mr. Peanuts by the throat. There is no 'spy' in team! He dunked the elephant into his bubbling aquarium, scattering the fish. "Stay out of my house! You hear me? Stay out!"

Suddenly, Mandrake froze. His eyed widened. Someone was behind him.

Grandma.

She stood at the door. Watching. She'd seen it all — the elephant, the aquarium, everything.

He eased away from the aquarium, letting Mr. Peanuts float like a dead man to the surface. "I... um... thought Mr. Peanuts needed a bath. He was starting to stink."

Grandma growled. Her face wrinkled... or wrinkled more.

Mandrake forced a smile. He looked utterly insane beneath his dark, rubbery, Russian surplus night-vision goggles. "You know... this is all probably just a phase. Kids my age have phases."

"What's that stupid thing on your face?" Grandma said.

Mandrake knees wobbled. "It's a... studying aid."

Grandma's jaundiced eyes shifted from Mandrake to his bed. She noticed — The Book!

Grandma's upper lip quivered and rattled the loose dentures beneath.

Mandrake pleaded, "It's... um... the Latin version? I barely understand a word of it."

Grandma snatched the memoir off the bed and turned to leave.

"Wait!"

She stopped at the door, her back to him, as if she couldn't bear to look into his traitorous eyes.

"That's a... um... library book," Mandrake called out stopping her again. "It needs to go back. Late charges and all."

She didn't move, either weighing the words or weighing the punishment. Finally, mercifully, she stomped off, taking the book with her. The muffled weight of her slippered feet pounded the hard wood floors and then —

SLAM! Her door hammered shut and rattled the walls. Mandrake stood frozen in the dark with his stupid goggles, mocked by the gentle bubbling of his fish tank.

Amateur Sleuth Rule #10

Sometimes a matchbook is just a matchbook.

THE MORNING SUN NEEDLED the still-floating corpse of Mr. Peanuts.

Mandrake scooped him out of the aquarium, squeezed some of the water out of him, slipped into the hall and ninja-walked to the front door. He called back up the stairs to his sleeping Grandma."Heading to school early today. Need to do some extra-credit and stuff. Going to walk. Good for the brain." He raced out the door trying to escape any hint of a response.

A dark storm hung on the horizon. Mandrake hustled to the sidewalk and trudged down the street with his backpack on his shoulders and the still-soaked polka-dot tucked under his arm. He didn't dare look back. Last night's encounter with Grandma weighed on him, but there more troublesome issues. The spying elephant in his room meant the Seven still didn't trust him. Mandrake planned to prove himself. He needed to find the missing Inspector.

But he wasn't good to do it sitting in a boring Algebra class. Yet, he knew he couldn't just ditch school, not with Vice Principal Lestrade on the case. And any whiff of trouble and Grandma would shut the whole thing down.

Mandrake arrived at Gunther Gates Middle School mere seconds before the rain began. He sprinted across the drab floor and checked the busted clock. It read 11:15. It always did. But judging from the glut of students rushing to and from their rusted lockers, he assumed the morning bell must have just sounded.

That's when he heard the chuckles and noticed the pointing fingers.

"Nice elephant, Mandrake," a girl with bows in her hair mocked. "Always had you for a pony and unicorn kid."

"Is today show-and-tell?" her sidekick with the pig-tails cackled.

Mandrake hid the water-logged plushy behind his back. "It's not mine. I just found it. It's a stray."

The girls giggled as they strolled past.

Mandrake tucked Mr. Peanuts under his shirt and rushed to his locker. Once away from judging eyes, he whipped his backpack around to shove the elephant inside.

But something was off. The backpack was already filled, and not by him. Mandrake had been in such a hurry, he didn't bother to pack his bag this morning.

It should have been empty but it wasn't.

He ripped open his bag and laid his eyes on the confiscated copy of "The Inspector Speaks."

"Hmmf." He scratched his head.

Grandma must have changed her mind about the banned book, secreted inside his room while he was sleeping, and slipped it into backpack.

Strange. Grandma wasn't stealthy.

But if it wasn't her, how else did the book end up in his bag?

Mandrake lifted the hardback and cracked it open. He quickly flipped the pages to Chapter 12: HOW I BROUGHT DOWN THE MANDRAKES.

The book stunk. Literally. The chemical smell of a magic marker filled his nostrils and brought a sting of tears to his eyes.

Black bars marred the page. The ink was still wet, its glossiness reflecting the fluorescent lights that hung above him. Various sentences and words were marked as one would with a highlighter.

Only it was the very opposite of a highlighter. Thick blocks of impenetrable black ink masked the type beneath, sanitizing the text for Mandrake's eyes like some top secret file declassified.

The school bell rang. Time for Algebra. Mandrake froze. He'd never been one to break the rules, but he had a city to save. He had no time for gym and recess. And certainly not for Algebra.

He turned and marched to the double-doors leading to the front parking lot. He was off to save the City! Nothing could stop him!

Guh! The neck of his shirt dug into his throat. Someone had him by the collar.

That someone was Vice Principal Lestrade. "Mr. Mandrake, I need a word."

Gulp. "Actually, I'm due in class."

"Then why are you heading toward the parking lot?"

"The school's a big place. I still get lost after all these years." Mandrake giggled. "Still need a GPS."

Lestrade dragged Mandrake outside. A slight drizzle had started, but Lestrade didn't seem to notice. "I know what you're up to, Mandrake. Falling in with the likes of Crash Brickfist."

Mandrake was astonished. He played it off. "Crash Who-fist?"

"Crash Brickfist. He was a student at this very school some twenty years ago. He and I got to know each other very well... until he was expelled."

"Fighting?"

"Fighting requires two participants. I'd say 'man-handling'. Mr. Simpkins didn't have a chance."

"Mr. Simpkins? The gym teacher? Didn't he play pro-football?"

"All-Pro and an ex-marine. He was never the same after getting the stuffing knocked out of him by an eleven-year-old." Lestrade narrowed his eyes. "Your father walked these halls, as well."

"Max Mandrake is not my father!" Mandrake softened a bit. "I mean technically he is. If you count DNA and stuff. But he's a criminal and a thief and goes against everything I stand for."

"Hm. He didn't like Latin either." Lestrade led Mandrake across the walkway and to the faculty parking lot.

The Vice Principal stopped at the curb. His shoulders drooped and his chin quivered. His reddened eyes focused on his dark black European sports car which sat in its usual reserved parking spot. Its sleek hand-waxed body was desecrated with red spray-painted words, and not the usual four letter kind one would expect in this kind of crime. These were scholarly type words more likely to be found on a crossword puzzle, not a bathroom wall.

"Surreptitious, Epitaph, Finesse. Epitaph."

Mandrake recognized them from his last vocabulary test. He'd gotten a C minus, so wasn't entirely sure if they were spelled right.

The words repeated all over the car like a punishment on a schoolroom chalkboard.

"What do you make of this?" Lestrade pointed at the hood of the car, which had a different set of graffiti letters — "OXOXOXOXOXOX".

"Hugs and kisses?" Mandrake guessed.

"That's XOXO. This is OXOX," Lestrade said.

"Kisses and hugs then?" Mandrake snapped a picture with his phone. "Or maybe it's someone from the varsity Tic-Tac-Toe team?"

"There's no such thing you idiot." Lestrade lips quivered. He looked like he was about to explode. "It's a tag. The Ox."

Mandrake shuddered. The mere mention of the bully's name sent fear down his spine. No one knew if Ox was his real name. It wasn't like any kid dared ask to see his birth certificate. At six feet tall and two hundred and fifty pounds, Ox towered over his puny classmates and teachers. He was a once-in-a-lifetime bully. He had skull tattoos and drove a Harley to middle-school. He had failed seventh grade five times and shaved with a switchblade. In a world of bullies, Ox was a super-bully.

"The Ox holds the all-time record for seventh grade detentions," Lestrade said through clenched teeth. "Nobody has more reason for revenge."

The rain beat harder, but Lestrade's simmering rage seemed to be an umbrella against it. "I want you to bring this thug to justice. I need evidence to expel him. Get me that and I'll owe you a huge favor."

Despite the downpour, warmth passed over Mandrake. He'd never gotten so much as a pat on the back or a 'thank you' note from his sleuthing exploits before. In the last twenty-four hours, he'd won entrance into an all-star group of super sleuths and gotten upgraded to a D plus on his Latin exam. And now this. Things were most definitely trending up.

"I think I might be able to help you here," Mandrake straightened his back to reflect his burgeoning confidence. "There's some stuff I need to get from the Baker Street Library. Detective stuff. Can I be excused from school for the day?"

Amateur Sleuth Rule #11

You'd be surprised how many cases involve dark & stormy nights - carry an umbrella.

Mandrake's rain-soaked sneakers squished down the hidden spiral staircase of the Baker Street Library. He'd just walked fifteen blocks through bucketing rain and flooded streets without an umbrella, or a hood, or even an old newspaper to take shelter beneath.

Wet was an understatement.

Even his underwear needed to be wrung out.

Mandrake scanned the abandoned subway tunnel that headquartered the Sleuthing Seven. He considered kicking off his soggy shoes, but this subterranean lair already had the damp stench of a swimming pool locker room. A few more moist footprints would do nothing but add to the mildewed ambience.

"Hello?" Mandrake's voiced echoed in the tomblike silence.

Even the apocalyptic thunder that terrorized Capital City above him couldn't penetrate the bunker-like walls of earth and concrete.

Mandrake wasn't sure what the standard working hours were for an All-Star team of crime-fighters. Did they take turns manning the fort in case they needed to jump into action? Did they sleep here? Did they meet once a week? Or once a month? Or only when crimes were committed?

Regardless, Wednesday at 10:48 a.m. was apparently not prime-time for the Sleuthing Seven.

Clickety-clack. Clickety-clack. Mandrake's neck snapped at the sound. Clickety-clack. Clickety-clack.

A blade of light escaped from underneath the conference doors.

"Crash? Pinot?" he called hopefully.

Still no answer, save for his own echo and the clickety-clacking.

Mandrake crept to the door. The repetitive sound went on uninterrupted. Whoever or whatever was making it didn't know he was here, and he intended to keep it that way.

He threaded the door's thin gap and slid into the conference room.

He looked up to see — MAX MANDRAKE!!!

He gasped.

It was just an old mug shot being displayed on one of the many monitors. Mandrake's face glowed with the blue-ish light as he gazed up at the gleaming imagery captured on the mounted monitors hung around the room. On screen there was evidence of an internet research session — magazines, blogs, video clips of old news programs. He scanned headlines: "MANDRAKES STEAL FOOTBALL STADIUM. CITY!" "MOST WANTED MAN ELECTED MAYOR", "CAST OF MOST POPULAR TV SHOW KIDNAPPED!" "FLEET OF ARMORED CARS HIJACKED", "EVERY TOY STORE ROBBED ON CHRISTMAS EVE"

Another set of monitors were themed around Mandrake's mother – stunt videos, acting headshots, and cold-reading audition videos of her trying out for Soap Operas and walk-on roles in cop-shows.

Most disturbing: one set of screens was filled with baby-pictures of Mandrake, including a totally embarrassing one of him naked in a bath tub.

At the center of all this, working a laptop like some maestro of multi-media, sat Abbey Prue.

Her back was to him. She gazed into the radiance of her bedazzled laptop, as her pony-tail danced to the tinny squeal of some girl pop anthem that leaked from the large sparkly headphones that hugged her meticulously coiffed mane.

Why was Abbey investigating Max Mandrake? It had been years

since Max had been locked away in prison. He posed no threat to the city and no challenge to the Seven.

Mandrake surmised she was digging up dirt on him. The same paranoia that led them to put a hidden camera in his stuffed elephant. They feared him. They felt he was in league with Max.

Mandrake fumed. He inched closer to sneak a peek at what was on her laptop screen.

Squish.

Mandrake's waterlogged socks betrayed his sneakiness. He hoped she didn't notice beneath the ear torture of sugary pop rock.

Her head went still. The jig was up —

"Hi, Abbey, what ya —"

Abbey flung around in her computer chair and whipped her knee-socked leg into Mandrake's. Before he could register what happened he was sprawled out on his back with a razor sharp bobby-pin perched at his racing jugular.

"Never sneak up on a Girl Scout," Abbey said.

"Words to live by," Mandrake said, remembering to breathe. "Whatcha listening to?"

Abbey returned her bobby-pin back into her perfectly-coiffed brown hair and eased back to her swivel chair. "Not that it's any of your business, but I'm learning Chinese."

"It sounded like music."

"To the untrained, perhaps. But I assure you, nothing goes into these ears that isn't food for the brain. And I don't do junk food." She turned back to her computer and closed it shut. The monitors around the room blinked off. "Why are you here? Don't you have show-and-tell or recess?"

"You know exactly why I'm here." Mandrake dramatically pulled Mr. Peanuts from his backpack and slammed him on the table, inadvertently making the toy's inner squeaker squeak.

Abbey stared at the toy, confused. "If you think I'm gonna play Elephant Tea Time, you've got the wrong girl detective."

"Don't pretend you don't know Mr. Peanuts." Mandrake mixed some super-hero gravitas into his voice. The sound came out a little more bed-time-puppet-show than he intended.

"I'm more of a giraffe girl."

Mandrake shook the doll in her face, "You may not know about this. But your friends do. The Seven are behind this!"

"The Seven?" She grabbed the elephant and a looked it in the eyes. "Oh! Of course! Now I remember! This is Crash Brickfist's first partner, Pinky Peanuts! They fight crime, then go home and have tickle fights and take bubble baths together —"

Mandrake snatched Mr. Peanuts away. "I'm not talking about the Elephant. I'm talking about what's inside the Elephant."

Mandrake threw the toy on the conference table and ripped into it with his bare hands.

"I don't know what kind of crazy stuffed toy autopsy you're trying to pull here, but I'm not gonna be the one to clean up all this fluff."

Mandrake dug deeper. His hands gouged the stuffing innards. And then he stopped. His fingers found something.

"Aha!" He revealed the cutest little itsy-bitsy cotton stuffed red velvet heart that said — MADE IN CHINA.

Mandrake's eyes went wide. Where was the spy camera? He'd heard the unmistakable whirring sound. The grind of the lens.

"Well, this was fun." Abbey gathered her laptop and threw on her coat. "There's a vacuum near the electric chair. Turn out the lights when you're done." She pushed past him and headed toward the spiral staircase.

"Wait! Where are you going?" Mandrake said. "Are you going to do some... sleuthing?"

"Uh... duh... I'm wearing my pencil skirt. Where else would I be going?" She shook her head. "Dork."

"Can I come along?"

"Uhhhh... let me think about that — NO." She marched up the steps.

Mandrake chased after her. "What if I could provide you with inside information?"

"Thanks, but I've learned about as much about Mr. Peanuts as I ever wanted to." She started up the stairs.

"What about inside family information?"

Abbey stopped. She slowly turned to him."Mandrake family information?"

"I'm part of the Seven. I want to help. But I can't help without someone letting me in. Somebody has to start telling me what's going on."

"Hmm. This family information, it's good?"

"Oh, it's good, real good." Mandrake faked confidence. "You wouldn't believe exactly how much I really know."

Abbey stared at him, long and hard, deciding. "Okay. But no stuffed things. I've got an image to protect."

"Really? I can come!" Mandrake shook with giddiness. "Where are we going?"

"The scene of the crime."

"The crime?"

"The place where Inspector Gates was last seen." She trotted up the steps. "You're not afraid of heights, are you?"

Amateur Sleuth Rule #12

**Make sure your medical insurance is paid up.
Same with your life insurance.**

ONCE AGAIN, MANDRAKE NEEDED a vomit strategy. The sleek black helicopter didn't have windows you could roll down, and the crammed cockpit didn't have a barf bucket. He didn't dare open the door and risk being electrified by the jagged daggers of lightning the helicopter weaved through. For now, holding his hand over his mouth and the peace of knowing he'd skipped breakfast would have to do.

Abbey strained to see through the shroud of precipitation. "I've only had my pilot's license for two weeks. It's much easier when you can see."

Mandrake's vision couldn't penetrate the spikes of rain that jack hammered the windshield. Every time he tried, he was greeted with an explosion of electric light and a bone-jarring cymbal crash of thunder. He prayed that they were high enough to avoid the skyscrapers of Capital City, and not too high to collide with a 747.

"You promised me information," Abbey prodded. "What do you know about your parents?"

Mandrake gulped hard. He had little knowledge outside of the famous headlines, and even most of those had been censored by his grandmother. But he didn't dare tell Abbey and risk her wrath. She needed all her wits about her to keep them from spiraling to a spectacular and wet death. "Um... well... they were criminals."

Thunder rumbled, as if God was clearing his throat and saying "liar... "

Abbey haruffed. "Seriously? That's all ya got?"

"Well, I was a baby when they were captured. I was found in diapers in the back of their car."

"Everybody knows that part. The chase. The bridge. The capture." Abbey softened. "Sorry about that by the way. You really hit the bad luck baby lottery. I mean, I've had problems with my Dad before. He's a small town sheriff. He stole the credit for all my brilliant detective work. But he never stole a nuclear bomb. Or killed my mom."

Turbulence buffeted the chopper. Abbey flipped switches, dipping the nose of the chopper, stabilizing the ride.

"Your father really pretended he solved all those cases?"

"Yeah. He said he was protecting me. He was protecting himself. Don't trust the adults. They hate when us kids run circles around them."

Mandrake sunk in his seat. Crash was always in the headlines for Mandrake's handiwork. Crash was always 'protecting' him.

"So, you got any clues to what happened to the Inspector?? It's your thing right?"

"My thing? I have a thing?"

"Come on. Remember, we've been watching you. We know what's really going on. It's why you're here."

"You mean the Nose."

Abbey laughed. "Is that what Crash called it? The Nose?"

"Called what?"

"Come on, you must know. Right?"

Wrong. Mandrake had no idea.

Abbey continued. "It's just the apple doesn't fall far from the tree. You think like one of them."

"Like who?"

"... like... a villain. A crook. A big bad. You've got bad-guy brain."

Mandrake winced like he just drank some chunky sour milk. Surely he must have heard her wrong. He had always used his powers to catch crooks. He despised evil and lawlessness. "That's ridiculous."

Abbey stared at him. "Is this part of it? Pretending not to know? Are you using your villain mojo on me?"

Mandrake stammered. "Where does this even come from?"

"Crash is the one who noticed it. The Farley brothers said you tested off the charts as a Criminal Mastermind. They say that's why you can see a villain's moves like some Grandmaster of chess. Seeing their schemes two or three steps ahead."

Mandrake reeled at the thought. Yes, he'd be the first to admit he was always ahead of... them. But one of them?! It was an insult of the highest level! The Seven just couldn't stand that he was better than them. First, they spy on him. Now they make up lies to justify why a kid was running circles around them at their own game.

"Oh, come on. It's not your fault. Professor Lung says it's genetic."

It always came back to that. Every time Mandrake walked down the school halls and kids laughed or pointed or whispered. When he was a toddler, parents pulled their kids from the playground and hustled them back to their mini-vans just to avoid swinging on the same swing set with a villain's child.

But the Sleuthing Seven were his people. Detectives. Sleuths. Crime fighters.

Mandrake shook his head. "That's why they brought me in, isn't it? To keep a close eye on me? In case I snapped. In case I turned into... him."

"Look, Mandrake, there's a part of this you still don't understand. They didn't want to tell you this, but your father is—"

Wind hammered the chopper, dropping it thirty feet before Mandrake could even open his mouth to scream. Warning alarms shrieked. The chopper rocked violently.

The apocalyptic gusts of wind and the helicopter's thumping blades waged war for control of the chopper. Mandrake glimpsed the lights ahead of them and finally realized their destination.

Crime Island.

"We're going to Crime Island?"

"We professionals call it The Capital City Correctional Institute for Exceptional Prisoners."

"I'm still going to call it Crime Island."

"The Inspector hates that name. He designed it, you know?"

"Of course," Mandrake said. He knew the history of the place. The Inspector had studied the greatest prison escapes in history. He cataloged all their flaws and turned them into escape-proof features. Most of the great jailbreaks involved some method of digging a hole through the bottom of one's cell and tunneling beneath prison gates. So the Inspector gathered Capital City's hottest architects and turned a bankrupt public works project to build a bridge into a 'floating prison'.

Mandrake peered through the rain and took in the long windowless rectangle of concrete suspended in mid-air like some building-sized swing by the thick bridge cables that housed the twenty most dangerous evil geniuses Capital City had ever known.

Among them, Max Mandrake.

The boy detective's stomach rumbled again. But this time the bile eruption had nothing to do with the weather.

Rain machine-gunned the windshield. Abbey nudged the chopper forward, weaving through the natural fireworks of lightning that suddenly erupted like a grand finale.

Floodlights were perched up in the high towers that anchored the cables of the bridge suspension. Mandrake knew that hidden behind the lights inside their crow's nests atop the towers, a battery of armed guards kept watch. Their weapons likely targeted both Abbey and him that very moment as they made their approach.

"What does the Inspector's disappearance have to do with Crime

Island?" Mandrake said as Abbey lowered them toward the helipad.

"It's the scene of the crime, silly. It takes a lot of red-tape cutting to get permission to come here. They don't even let guards inside without a court order. This is the Seven's first chance to really have a look."

"Why aren't the rest of the Seven here?"

"They're busy with some incident in the city. They tend to give me the 'kid jobs' — researching, conducting witness interviews, pouring through ransom notes or whatever. The Seven like to say we're all equals but the reality is they don't let us 'juniors' do the dangerous stuff."

"Like flying helicopters in torrential downpours," Mandrake said.

"Can you see the helipad?" Abbey asked.

"I can't see anything," Mandrake said.

"Well, it's got to be down there somewhere." Abbey focused on keeping the chopper steady. "We haven't had a real case since I've joined. The Sleuthing Seven put all the master criminals behind bars before I ever signed up. It's about time we got some real action."

Suddenly, the chopper lost all control. Spiraling down. Abbey wrestled with the controls as they spun wildly. "Here goes nothing."

Abbey dropped the chopper... A tremendous free fall and then — SLAM — metal met concrete. Mandrake's teeth crunched together from the jolt. His eyes voluntarily squinched shut.

A roar of thunder snapped Mandrake's eyes open like a screeching alarm clock. He tried to jump out of his seat, but was pinned down by the buckle. The straps bit into his arms, but the pain was welcome — he was alive!

"Wow... I'm really getting better with my landings." Abbey let the rotors above them peter out and unbuckled her safety belt. She popped open her door and unfurled the cutest little yellow umbrella, strolling off, leaving Mandrake alone to calm his jackrabbiting pulse.

Mandrake hopped out and was instantly assaulted by bullets of water from above. He shuffled after Abbey, keeping his eyes on the bright yellow umbrella lest he lose her in the low visibility.

A drenched warden in a traffic-cone orange rain poncho lumbered toward them. He frowned when he glimpsed the underwhelming detective duo. "So you're the hot-shot detective force we were told to expect," he said. "Do your parents know you're here?"

"Do your parents know you let the most notorious prisoner in Capital City escape from your prison?" Abbey snapped back.

The Warden grumbled — touché — and ushered them towards a large metal submarine-style hatch.

Mandrake froze, as he realized what Abbey's retort truly meant.

The most dangerous criminal in Capital City, if not the world over, was now at large.

Max Mandrake had escaped!

Mandrake vomited.

Amateur Sleuth Rule #13

Most cases aren't Whodunits, they're Whybothers.

THE HATCH ABOVE THEM SLAMMED shut, silencing the raging storm. Not even the rain that pelted the roof registered. This prison was air tight.

"Where are the other guards?" Mandrake said as he followed Abbey and the Warden down the long metal ladder.

"Guards?" The Warden chuckled. "This prison doesn't need guards."

They stepped off the ladder. Mandrake's wet shoes squeaked on the metal beneath them. Dozens of round holes dotted the floor. They reminded Mandrake of the ones he sank putts into at the Jurassic Putt Mini-golf downtown, except deeper, shadowy.

The Warden tapped a wall-sized touch screen computer at the far end of the otherwise empty room. "Crime Island is the world's first guard-less prison. I manage the various inner workings of the whole shebang right from my control room, but otherwise we don't use guards. Makes for a pretty boring Christmas party."

The Warden navigated through a series of menus and screens. "Inspector Gates determined the number one risk of prison escape was accomplices... and birthday cakes. You can't bribe somebody that's not here. And you can't smuggle a metal file in a pistachio cupcake. Way too small, yet still deliciously festive. Oh, please step on the feet." The Warden nodded to five sets of colored footprints sunken a few inches deep into the center of the floor.

Abbey and Mandrake stepped into the prints. Bloop! Their feet registered in the far right side of the computer screen. Bloop! Weight.

Bloop. Pulse rate. Bloop. Make and model of tennis shoes.

Fwish. A small metal tray slid out from a wall compartment. The Warden grabbed it and turned back to Mandrake and Abbey. "You can't enter the prison with any weapons or electronic devices. If you're packing heat, put it in the receptacle." Abbey filled the tray with her bobby pins, saddle shoes, purse, lipstick, chewing gum, earrings... and then after thinking, her retainer.

The Warden turned to Mandrake. "What about you, son? Any bobby pins or dental work?"

Mandrake held his phone up. "What about this? I use it to take notes."

The Warden held up his hand. "Keep it. The prison is cut off from any kind of radio, satellite, or cellular communication. Just don't throw it to anyone."

The tray with Abbey's stuff slurped back inside the wall and snapped shut. The Warden pressed a single virtual button on the computer screen — "Initiate Frisk-o-Matic."

The ceiling lights dimmed. An engine vroomed. Gears inside the walls and floor cranked. The sound built, then roared.

"Assume the position," a computer voice boomed from hidden speakers.

The Warden stepped on footprints next to Mandrake and Abbey.

The computer voice continued, "Frisk begins in three, two, one..."

Large metal hands attached to articulated springs shot out from the round holes around their feet like snakes jumping out of a can of prankster peanut brittle. Two hands frisked their lower legs while another explored their backs, yet another shot down from the ceiling and mussed their hair.

The touch screen cycled through a library of threats the fingers were frisking for – guns, knives, throwing stars, nun-chuks, boomerangs, bazookas, battle axes, slingshots —"

Mandrake bit his lip as the robo-fingers went to work under his arm pits. He was crazy ticklish but didn't want to seem unprofessional.

Then the Warden cackled. "Best part of the job!" He said, tears pouring out of his eyes.

Then Abbey.

Mandrake finally followed suit.

They cackled like helpless toddlers under the assault of a full on tickle ambush.

Anvils, pianos, War & Peace hardbacks, brass knuckles, enemas, boomboxes, banana peels—

"Banana peels?" Mandrake asked through uncontrollable guffaws.

"In the right hands... " the Warden said between squeals.

Paperclips, snowballs, fruitcakes, whoopee cushions, celery sticks, golf clubs, ping pong paddles, poodles, licorice, clown shoes...

The computer rattled off more threats as the cyber-fingers frenetically searched, poking Mandrake's ears, pig nosing his nostrils, even finger-scrubbing his gums and pulling back his eyelids.

... Cobras, air horns, silly string, firecrackers, rocks, paper, scissors, superglue, glitter, hot sauce, crab claws, lawn darts, spitballs, tarantulas, croquet mallets...

The engines revved down. The fingers went still. The long limbed arms retracted to their rabbit holes.

"Frisk-o-Matic complete," the robotic voice droned.

The Warden wiped the laughter-induced waterworks from his ruddy cheeks. "I might've peed a little."

Abbey's typical military precision hair looked like it was run through a blender of hairspray by the Bride of Frankenstein's beauty consultant. "No pictures, Mandrake."

The floor lowered beneath them. It gave the impression that the room was stretching. The screens, hatches and ceiling above them stayed in place as they distanced themselves and sank to the lower levels of the prison.

They stopped with a clang that buckled Mandrake's knees. A pneumatic hiss sizzled through the air.

The Warden waved at a newly revealed doorway. "Welcome to Crime Island."

They pushed inside, entering an office about the size of Mandrake's bedroom. On its walls, clunky old 1950's-era black and white televisions monitored every inch of the prison.

Abbey planted herself in front of one. Using the glassy reflection, she frantically salvaged the tornado twist of hair that rested on her head.

"So, what's with the whole antique A/V Club vibe?" Mandrake tapped a thick glass screen with his finger. Ting. Ting. Ting. Static energy radiated off the machine, tingling the hairs on Mandrake's hand. "Budget-cuts?"

"Hardly," the Warden adjusted the large rabbit-eared antenna on one of the sets."These dinosaurs cost ten times as much to run and service as modern tech. The Inspector insisted on an all analog design. Everything is one hundred percent hacker proof. No computers. No internets —"

"— no hairbrushes," Abbey said as she put the finishing touches on her hair.

"Must get boring." Mandrake took in the room.

"I've got my crosswords," the Warden said. "No pencils — thanks to the Frisker — but plenty of crosswords."

The Warden stepped over to a stack of cardboard boxes filled with food and began to stuff sandwiches and juice boxes inside small plastic cylinders. "Sorry, it's lunchtime for the inmates."

"So," Abbey cased the room. "Crime Island is supposed to be escape-proof, yet, there's a prisoner that's gone missing. Any ideas?"

"It's a stumper." The Warden stuck one of the food cylinders into a tube identical to the kind used at a bank. He pressed a button and the cylinder was sucked inside and torpedoed away. "Even if zero-zero-one could get out of his cell, I have no idea how he'd get off the Island. He'd have to get through that door, get by me, go through the frisking machine, figure out a way to fake my handprint to use the elevator, and then unlock the hatch. Then, once you're outside, it's not like you could fly away."

Mandrake cocked a brow. "What if you had a jetpack? Or a hang-glider? Or a bungee cord?"

Abbey's eyes narrowed on him. "See... that's just a way a villain would think."

Mandrake blushed. He ducked away, pretending to read his connectionless phone. "Max Mandrake was known for his evil inventions. He shut down the city once with weather control technology."

The Warden nodded. "He also was a master of disguise! He created a technology to disguise himself as anyone he wanted by pressing a button on his wrist watch. Called it the Max-A-Morpher. Boy, I'd like to get that for the next Halloween party."

Abbey shook her head. "He couldn't just jetpack off, though. Wouldn't the guards in the tower see him?"

"Most definitely," the warden nodded. "They were already on high-alert after the power-surge —"

"Power surge?" Abbey said. "When did that happen?"

"It was right after Inspector Gates arrived. He came in the same helicopter you're flying," the Warden said. "Said he was here on a matter of City-wide security. He requested to speak with zero-zero-one immediately but asked that our usual sound surveillance equipment be turned off. It's policy to keep the video recording at all times but we accommodated him with the audio. Apparently, he suspected a leaker in our midst. A rat. Rumor had it the leaker was among his own colleagues." The Warden glared at Mandrake.

"I'm not a leaker," Mandrake snapped back. "I have amazing bladder control."

The Warden crossed his arms. "That's what they all say... well... not the bladder part, the first part."

"So, this power surge... ?" Abbey reminded him.

"It happened while the Inspector was conducting his interrogation inside Mandrake's cell. I was watching them on my screen right here." He tapped the monitor with the empty cell. "Sometimes when the sound's down I like to make voices for the people on the screens. Make a little TV show out of it. Funny stuff. Sometimes I just do fart noises."

Mandrake and Abbey shot him confused looks.

"Uh... anyway, there was a power grid malfunction at the base of the bridge supports. The surge knocked out all electricity to the prison. Total blackout. We don't have windows in here — big escape risk, windows. Toilets too, by the way, but we had to install toilets. I think it might be a law or something."

"How soon was it till the lights came back on?" Mandrake asked.

"We flipped to emergency power in less than five seconds — but when we did, inmate zero-zero-one had vanished."

"Vanished?" Mandrake said. "You mean... like... a wizard?"

"There weren't any chants or long beards or pointy hats. More like a guy in a tuxedo pulling a rabbit out of the hat kind of deal," the Warden said."Actually, I hate magic. Though I like balloon animals. Except for the squeaky sound. Makes my teeth hurt."

"So was there a puff of smoke? A flash? Or did he leave a pile of empty clothes?" Abbey asked.

"No. That would've been pretty cool though, right? Still, it's a total head-scratcher. All of our locking and cage mechanisms remained sealed shut. It would take a truck to move those doors. Without electrical power, they don't open. You'd have to walk through walls to escape."

"And what did the Inspector do?" Abbey asked.

"He was awfully surprised. He searched around the cell, but took off in a hurry. He said something about stopping him before it's too late."

"Too late for what?" Mandrake asked.

"Beats me." The Warden lifted a large black videotape. The kind that went extinct almost 30 years ago. "Here's the Betamax. Don't show it to anyone. The Inspector said he didn't want to start a panic."

Mandrake reached for it but Abbey snatched it away and wedged it inside her purse. "We need to investigate the cell. We're in a hurry. Junior's up against curfew."

"The cell? You're going in there?" He pointed to the thick steel door at the back of the room.

Abbey smiled. "That's the plan."

"It's your funeral." The Warden sat at a large panel of buttons and knobs. "I control the opening and closing of cell doors from here."

"You're not coming?" Mandrake asked.

"I couldn't if I wanted to, and I don't. It's a failsafe. I need to hold the button from here to keep the door open. It's so no one inside the prison can open the doors," the Warden said. "Besides, I have a Sudoku to stare at."

He hit a large red button.

Inside the walls around the door frame, heavy gears clanked and clanged. Cables and chains rattled. The door rose from the floor and retracted into the wall revealing a long corridor that Mandrake recognized from the Internet — the prison block nicknamed Crime Alley.

"Better hurry," the Warden said, lifting his puzzle book. "The door is on a timer."

Abbey grabbed Mandrake's hand and yanked him through.

SLAM. The heavy door guillotined shut behind them.

Mandrake's heart twitched. He took a deep breath and gazed ahead. Dim ceiling lights bread-crumbed the path in front of them.

"You should stay here," Abbey said.

"You said you'd show me the crime scene."

"I said 'I'd take you along.' I did. But it's time to get some real work done, and I don't need you in my way."

"You know this is my thing," Mandrake said.

"Oh please." She laughed and rolled her eyes at the same time. Mandrake was starting to wonder if that was her thing.

"I can help you here, Abbey. And if I do, you'll get all the credit."

"Credit? As if I need your hand-me-downs." She straightened and crossed her arms. Despite her feigned offense, she wasn't rolling her eyes or making that face. "But I was the one smart enough to bring you. Takes an expert to identify an expert, after all."

She looked at him, then the hall, then him. "Okay. But keep your eyes straight and follow me. The most dangerous people in the world are locked up in here. Try not to pee yourself." Abbey launched straight down Crime Alley.

Amateur Sleuth Rule #14

**If something completely defies
the rules of logic...
consider that the rules might be wrong.**

THE MOST VILLAINOUS MADMEN in the world glared at Mandrake through their glass cages. The boy detective didn't dare make eye contact. He kept his eyes forward and followed Abbey. His attuned senses felt their stares bearing down on him like a microwave's rays on a helpless frozen burrito.

A spindly man tapped bulletproof glass drawing Mandrake's attention. "An apple day won't keep me away," he hissed.

Mandrake recognized the 'catch phrase' and the corpse-pale face. The Surgeon was once the go-to brain butcher at Capital General Hospital, until his license was revoked for harvesting human organs and modifying his own intelligence through self-surgery. His efforts gave him unparalleled genius but left him scarred and deranged. The Inspector ultimately collared him for gut-jacking the Mayor's innards and ransoming the city to put them back in.

"Take two and call me in the morning," he sinisterly whispered.

Mandrake quickened his pace.

"You're sweating, aren't you?" Abbey crinkled her nose. "Villains can smell fear. And by extension they can smell your sweat-stained pits. Suck your sweat in, Mandrake. Think dry thoughts."

Mandrake visualized Death Valley and Scones and Melba toast but his hyper-awareness fueled his perspiration. "Maybe we can go over the case... to take my mind off my sweat glands."

Abbey threw her hands. "There's not much. Inspector Gates was last seen by the Warden."

"What about the helicopter?" Mandrake said. "Where did you find it? At the library?"

"It was abandoned at the soccer field behind Capital High School."

"That's a few blocks from my house." Mandrake's head whipped to Abbey but unfortunately, he looked right past her to a face squished against the glass in a hideous expression of childlike menace.

Even deformed, Mandrake recognized the boy from the reruns he and Grandma watched every night at six pm over dinner — Arnold the Terror.

Arnold wasn't his real name, it was the menacing adolescent character he played for eight seasons on the Emmy award nominated series Arnold the Terror. It had been almost twenty years since the show was abruptly cancelled due to declining viewership, yet Arnold still had that exact same baby-face. And he hadn't grown. He was shorter than Mandrake by almost a foot. He didn't look older than seven. A creepy seven. A master of media, Arnold had once hijacked all the local television stations and ransomed them off during a Must-See-TV-Thursday.

"No autographs, punk." Arnold sat back in his bed.

Mandrake scurried ahead.

"You're not going to puke are you? You look kind of puke-ey." Abbey asked, keeping her eyes straight and her stride consistent.

"I really hadn't considered it until just now."

"Well don't. They feed off that, you know? Metaphorically. Mostly they eat cream-chipped beef. So gross."

BAM! A fist slapped on a cell to Mandrake's left. "Help me! They put a microchip in my brain! I need your help."

A pale face, behind thick glasses and topped off with greasy unkempt hair smooshed the glass. The Programmer! A villainous hacker so technologically treacherous he could cripple nations with a double-click. He once encrypted the entire Internet then sold off his decryption app for billions.

"Act like you've been there!" Abbey yanked Mandrake's face forward. "They can't get to you. They're behind three feet of bullet-proof glass."

Mandrake turned his glance to the opposite wall and gazed right at the Maniac Brothers, Pyro and Klepto. Like always, they stood shoulder to shoulder — they were conjoined twins — glaring coldly at Mandrake.

"Stop looking at them." Abbey yanked Mandrake ahead to Max Mandrake's empty cell.

He stared inside. "Can't we go in?"

"The guard can't open the door." Abbey sighed. "He doesn't have that authority."

"Then what do we do?"

"Just stare in. Like a museum." Abbey squished her face against the glass and peered in.

Mandrake followed her lead - THUNK — hitting his head a little too hard against the glass.

She shot him a look. "Rookie."

Mandrake blushed. He could feel a welt forming on his head, but didn't want to mention it. Abbey already thought he was worthless. He needed to come up with something big to impress her.

He gazed at the small table at the center of the room. A coffee cup sat on a newspaper. The paper's headline from a few months ago read "NO MORE VILLAINS."

Would Max Mandrake have been insulted by such a headline? Challenged to reverse the tide? Was the media daring him to return?

"Haven't cracked the case yet?" Abbey chided. "So much for The Nose."

His eyes fluttered. The Nose, indeed. He smelled something.

Something unusual in this carefully-controlled environment. Something sweet. Fruit? A peach? He perched his nostrils against the mesh of holes that allowed air to circulate within the cell and sniffed wildly.

"Okay, this is getting embarrassing," Abbey said. "If you start licking the glass, I'm gonna lose it."

Mandrake straightened and put the bloodhound impersonation on hold. He stared inside, searching for that clue everyone else missed. "Decaf soy latte. Skinny. But it wasn't the prisoner's, it was —"

"The Inspector's. Yeah, I can read the writing on the side of the cup too. What else ya got, Mr. Bad-Guy Brain?"

He ignored the crack and scanned the walls where several paintings hung. Photo-realistic masterpieces of every shape and size depicting cityscapes, other inmates, bowls of fruit. "Max Mandrake did these?"

"He's good. A few of his works got into the Capital Museum of Art last year. Amazing stuff. Especially considering the prison doesn't allow brushes. These are all finger-paintings. I guess he doesn't get to see any beaches anymore, so he paints them."

Mandrake decided not to clue her in to his own artistic ability and his acceptance to a fancy art school. She had enough ammunition.

"Is that your mom?" Abbey asked.

Mandrake followed her gaze to a framed painting of a young woman, late twenties, athletic build, close-cropped hair. She showed no hint of a smile, only a blank gaze and a flat expression and haunting eyes. Green like Grandma's.

Abbey continued on. "I watched that video where she base-jumped off the Capital Bank tower. She was like a movie stunt woman or something, wasn't she?"

"Yeah," Mandrake said, still locked on the painting. There was something so familiar about the woman, even though they'd never really met.

"I wonder why she gave that up?"

"Stunt work is a thankless job," Mandrake said, realizing he could be talking about amateur sleuthing. "Stunt people risk their lives, do all the hard work, then the movie stars get all the cred."

"Too bad. She was good." Abbey peered over his shoulder. "So, what's your nose tell ya?"

Mandrake tapped the glass. "What if after the Inspector came in, the door didn't shut somehow? Or it was open a crack."

"Buzzzzzzzz. Wrong." She honked like the sound of a TV game show. "The glass door was shut and secured behind Inspector Gates the entire time."

"Maybe when the lights went out —"

"Buzzzzzzzz. Wrong again. The gears use electricity. They don't open without power. She pointed her thumb back to the hall. "The security tape confirms it."

"Well, what about tra—"

"—trap doors?" Abbey finished his sentence. "They molded these cells as single large blocks then pieced them together. Twenty feet thick on each side. A bomb wouldn't even make a dent in it."

"Seems excessive."

"More like meticulous. It's Inspector Gates we're talking about here." Abbey tapped on the wall-size glass that separated them from the cell. "The shatterproof glass is three feet thick. The room is so airtight, they have to pump air through those vents." Abbey nodded to the ceiling. A tiny duct loomed over them, not big enough for a man, or even an infant to crawl through. "And even if Max managed to get out of his cell, he'd need transport back to the city. The fall is certain death... and there's nowhere to climb."

"Well, there must be something." Mandrake's eyes drifted to the wall beside Max's bed. Taped to it was a wrinkly piece of paper filled with writing. It resembled a grocery list, or maybe a villainous ToDo list. He couldn't read the words with his prescription-assisted eyes, so he pulled out his phone and switched to camera mode. He zoomed in on the jagged loose leaf. He read the handwriting at the top:

THE 44 RULES OF AMATEUR SLEUTHING

Abbey spied over his shoulder. "What idiocy is this?"

"It's like a guide to detective work." Mandrake read aloud. "Rule number one – The Butler didn't do it. Butlers are gentlefolk. Consider the maid. Rule number two – When naming cases always use alliteration —"

"Rule number 3. Stop. Now." Abbey massaged her temples. "I'm losing IQ points."

Mandrake snapped a picture. "Anything this stupid must be a clue."

Abbey sighed. "Yeah. That could be rule seventy-eight."

Mandrake widened the zoom and took a picture of the entire cell. He noticed something else. On the floor by the table sat two black and white photos.

He pinch zoomed, enlarging the image. The photos were surveillance style, the type taken using long-lenses from dark cars with tinted windows. His eyes fell on the carefully manicured bushes, the two story house with the black shutters and pink flamingos that stood sentry by the porch.

"That's my house!" Mandrake pinch zoomed on the second photo. This one was a close-up shot through a window of Mandrake and his grandmother on their living room couch watching television.

"I know what Max is after." Mandrake turned to Abbey. "Me."

AMATEUR SLEUTH RULE #15

Never, ever, say 'the game is afoot'.
Just. Don't.

THE CHOPPER'S SKIDS TOUCHED DOWN on the pitcher's mound, kicking up a cyclone of rain-soaked mud. Abbey cut the rotors and turned to Mandrake. "So. This was fun. We should do it again."

Mandrake stepped out. His white shoes sank into the quicksand of mud. The thunderstorm had settled to a drizzle but not before turning the infield into a diamond of brown sludge.

"If you hurry you can catch the bus," Abbey said.

Mandrake looked through the fenced backstop behind home plate and saw his fellow students climbing onto their respective buses. If Mandrake hustled, he could avoid the long, cold walk home. "Abbey, there's something I'm wondering about."

"Well, spit it out. I ain't a mind reader. Not a confirmed mind reader at least. But I've had my moments."

"What night did the escape happen at Crime Island?"

"Oh. Uh. Gosh. I don't know." Abbey said. "I was pleating my skirts. Must've been Monday."

"Monday? You're sure?"

"Yeah. Definitely Monday. We were all called in early that evening. Around five, maybe six o'clock."

Mandrake stroked the prickles of his peach fuzzed chin. "Monday was the night I caught the Bearded Bank Bandit."

"Oh?" Abbey's face reddened. "I didn't realize that. That's some coincidence." She turned back to the controllers to avoid his gaze.

Mandrake's mind raced. "If Max Mandrake had gone fugitive and the Inspector was missing in action — wouldn't Crash have more important things to do than go chasing a bank bandit?"

Abbey fired up the chopper's rotors. "Sorry, didn't quite catch that last bit. Anyhoo, gotta boogie. Chopper's running on fumes and it ain't gonna fuel itself up, you know."

She reached over to shut the door but Mandrake grabbed it. "Why would Crash be wasting his time with me?"

Abbey snapped on a pair of noise canceling headphones. "Sorry. Can't hear. Can't even read lips because of the dirt-nado out there."

"I'm not letting go of this door until you answer me!" Mandrake yelled over the rotors.

Abbey dug the clunky plastic security video out of her purse. "You want this?"

Mandrake's eyes widened.

"Fetch!" She threw it past him and into a muddy puddle. He turned to get it.

WHAM! She slammed the chopper door shut and began to take off.

Mandrake called out as he shielded himself from the dirt-nado of wet earth. A clump of mud flew into his mouth. He choked as Abbey piloted off into the sky.

Behind him, he could hear the squealing brakes of the horribly-maintained school buses as they cruised up the hill and vanished into the streets and neighborhoods beyond.

Mandrake fished the video from the muck, hoisted his backpack on both shoulders and plodded through the soupy field. He had a long walk ahead of him, and the most dangerous criminal in capital city was out there somewhere, hunting him.

AMATEUR SLEUTH RULE #16

There's no such thing as Occam's Shaving Cream.

THE STREETLIGHTS BUZZED AWAKE AS Mandrake sprinted across his front lawn, hurdled the porch stairs and whipped his front door open. He gently eased the door shut, not making a sound, and locked the door.

He peered out the curtains. No sign of Max. For now he was safe.

"Miss the bus?" Grandma said, causing Mandrake to scream. She loomed over him, arms folded across her chest.

"Uh... yeah. I was studying." He fought to catch his breath and pretend everything was cool. "Good times. Didn't even hear the bell ring."

Her eyes drooped to his mud-splattered outfit. "Must have taken a short-cut through a pig-sty."

"Oh. Yeah. Funny story. I got caught in one of those flash mud-storms."

"Hmmm," Grandma said.

"It's rare. But it happens. Rarely. But yes."

She locked Mandrake in one of her signature double-barreled glares.

He peeled off his coat, trying to avoid her gaze. "Or maybe it fell off the back of a truck. You know, one of those dirt delivery trucks. On its way to one of those dirt super stores. Dirt Depot."

His lying needed serious work. He faked a yawn. "Well, I'm bushed. I'm just going to go clean up and then off to nighty-night." He shuffled toward the steps.

"Stop!" Her shrill voice froze him.

She turned him around. "A life of secrets and lies is no life at all."

"Of course, I uh... not sure what you mean?"

She snorted. "Life is about sharing, not sneaking."

"I share. Just... not with you. I share with my friends."

"Your friends? And who might they be? Crash Brickfist? Or the Police? Or maybe that old priest at the library?"

"Well... " Mandrake fumbled for a response. "They're not my only friends."

"They're not your friends at all. Friends don't have an agenda."

Mandrake's face burned. Who was she to judge? It wasn't like she was Miss Popularity at the Senior Center or anything.

She pointed a fat finger at him. "You're a child. You should be having fun. Not doing others' dirty business."

"Who says 'dirty business' isn't fun?"

"Hmpf." Grandma scowled. "You sound like your father."

"Or like your daughter?"

Grandma flinched.

Mandrake stopped. He should shut up. He shouldn't cross this threshold. "Maybe you don't know as much about kids as you think? After all, you did raise a super villain!"

Grandma's lips quivered. He'd scored with that one.

"Besides, I'm nothing like her. I'm one of the good guys."

Grandma's voice trembled, "Good guys don't lie to the ones they love."

"Good guys need to do good things! If it were up to you, I wouldn't be able to. I'd be in Poodle Springs! Drawing bowls of fruit!" It was Mandrake's turn to point at her. "What I do is what separates me from... them."

"No, child. It's what makes you the same. Your father was a member of that super secret library club, too."

This time Mandrake flinched. "You're lying!" But somehow he knew she wasn't. She wouldn't lie to him. Not about this. He could barely breathe. He needed to get out of here. He needed to be away from her, from everyone.

Mandrake sprinted to his room and slammed the door behind him, rattling the large magnifying glass off its perch on the high-shelf. It hit the floor, fracturing its lens down the center.

He slammed down his backpack and crawled beneath the covers. Fire coursed through his veins like he'd just stepped off the wildest roller-coaster in existence.

The old floor creaked in the hall. He imagined Grandma's bunioned feet hobbling up the stairs. She was probably headed for his room, wanting to talk, to make everything all right again.

And as angry as he was, right now, he needed her, more than ever.

Click. The lights in the hallway snapped off, followed by a prolonged silence.

Five minutes went by, then ten.

She wasn't coming.

He grabbed his backpack and pulled out Mr. Peanuts.

It didn't matter that his plush pink chest was torn up and he was now missing most of his stuffing. He cuddled him close.

Tonight, he needed something to hold on to.

AMATEUR SLEUTH RULE #17

Be advised: a MacGuffin is not a breakfast sandwich.

FOR THE SECOND STRAIGHT MORNING, Mandrake skipped the school bus. He'd decided to take the wheel of his own destiny and steer it right to the Baker Street Library.

He'd spent the night mulling this course of action and the wee hours of the morning crafting his Letter of Resignation. Crafting might be an over-exaggeration. It simply read — "I quit." — with his signature on the bottom.

He sealed it, along with the golden library card, in a business envelope and labeled it "To Whom It May Concern."

Mandrake marched past the bronze bloodhounds, up the granite steps, and to the front entrance. He slid the envelope under the slim crack at the bottom of the giant-sized double doors.

The deed was done. He was now officially a solo act. With a spring in his step, he turned his back to the library and the Seven.

The enormous library doors rumbled open.

"Aren't you supposed to be in school?" Mandrake recognized the French accent — Pinot.

"I'm heading there now." Mandrake replied without turning.

"What is this envelope?"

Mandrake didn't have to turn to know what he was talking about. "It's a letter of resignation."

"It's written in crayon," Pinot said.

Mandrake turned up his hands apologetically. "I didn't have any pens. It felt a little more official than pencil."

Pinot slid on his reading glasses and read the note. "Your resignation is rejected."

"Rejected? Is that even allowed?"

"Of course it is. Garcon stupide! Now, go to school." Pinot retreated back inside.

"No!" Mandrake stomped his foot. "I reject your rejection."

Pinot ripped the letter and the envelope into tidy little pieces. "One doesn't resign from The Sleuthing Seven."

"What about Max Mandrake? Didn't he resign?"

"Oh la vache!" Pinot froze mid-rip. "Is this why you wish to jeter le'ponge?"

"I don't want to 'jeter' anything." Mandrake said. "I want to quit! I'm sick of doing all the work and letting others take credit."

"There's more to this than that."

"Like the fact that you don't even trust me. That you think I'm going to become some dangerous villain."

Pinot wagged a finger, beckoning Mandrake into the library as he scanned the perimeter, likely looking for anyone who may have overheard the exchange.

Mandrake followed him inside, letting the doors shut behind him.

"Your papa was Inspector Gates' protégé." Pinot strolled to a window and peered through a venetian blind. "He was the most gifted deductive mind the Inspector had ever seen. But he was young. Too young. His success went to his head. He quit school just a few days after his sixteenth birthday. He wanted to focus on battling the criminals of Capital City. "

"What happened? How did he go... bad?"

"He felt the Inspector was holding him back. One day, he stormed in here, much like you did today, and turned in his library card." Pinot turned back to Mandrake. "You could do great good."

"Or great harm." Mandrake smirked. "You wanted to make sure I didn't become my father."

"You share his talents. It was my fervent desire that you would not share his career aspirations. When Max Mandrake turned to crime, it took Inspector Gates and the entire society every ounce of sleuth-ability to defeat him.... and it cost your mother her life."

"Who is to say you didn't make him the way he is?"

Pinot sneered and shuffled. The accusation clearly made him uncomfortable. "You could be in peril. At least consider staying until we find Max Mandrake."

Mandrake turned to the door and grabbed the large knob. "If anyone is going to find Max Mandrake, it'll be me. And I won't do it hiding out in some old library." He stormed out.

"Wait!" Pinot rushed after him. "There's something else —"

Mandrake had heard enough. He slammed the door behind him and hurried down the steps.

The dong of the clock tower signaled the top of the hour. It was 9 a.m.

Mandrake was late for school.

AMATEUR SLEUTH RULE #18

While a MacGuffin is not a breakfast sandwich, a breakfast sandwich could be a MacGuffin... though it is rare.

"STOP!" MANDRAKE SHOUTED AS he poked his head through the doorway of Vice Principal Lestrade's office.

Lestrade's crooked finger perched over the "8" on the phone's touch-pad — the final digit of Grandma's phone number.

"Don't do it!" Mandrake shouted in desperation. "I forgot to set my clock back."

"You're three hours late," Lestrade said, his finger nearing the button like a super-villain about to launch a missile.

"I forgot three years in a row," Mandrake said unconvincingly.

Lestrade sneered and punched the final phone digit.

Mandrake's heart did a drum solo. The ringing of his home phone bled from the receiver. Mandrake's great new solo career was about to come to an abrupt halt. If his Grandma found out he had been cutting school she would ground him for life.

"You can't do this!" Mandrake said.

Lestrade raised his cold eyes to meet Mandrake's. "Why not?"

Mandrake's own gaze whipped away, escaping the Vice Principal's cold stare. He settled on an exotic car calendar on the wall behind Lestrade's shoulder. "Your car! I was late because of your car!"

On the third ring. Grandma picked up, "I don't care what you're selling?"

Lestrade covered the mouthpiece. "You got the Ox?"

"Socks?!!" Grandma barked on the other end. "You're telemarketing socks? What's this world coming to?"

"I don't know who did it," Mandrake said. "But I know where they'll be."

"Where?" Lestrade hung up.

"Detention." Mandrake sat down and put his feet up on the desk.

Lestrade slapped them away. "You want to go to detention?"

Mandrake leaned forward and lowered his voice. "I couldn't just show up in detention. Those delinquents would sniff me out in a heartbeat. I need to go undercover. This whole public lateness thing — is just part of the plan."

Lestrade stared him down, considering.

"I'll be your spy. Working on the inside." Mandrake picked up a pencil. "Write me up a detention slip."

"You sure about this, son? You won't survive a minute there."

"It's the only way I'm going to crack your case. Besides, I'm tougher than you think." Mandrake tried snapping the pencil to prove his strength. But it wouldn't break. He gritted his teeth and bent it with all his might, but the stupid pencil wouldn't give.

Lestrade snatched it away and reached into the pocket of his white short-sleeved shirt and pulled out a stack of yellow detention slips. "It's your funeral." Lestrade scribbled out a slip for Mandrake

"You've got 'til the end of detention." He ripped the slip off the pack and handed it to Mandrake. "You either give me proof of who desecrated my sacred baby by the end of the day ... or I'm calling your Grandmother and putting an end to you. Once and for all."

Amateur Sleuth Rule #19

**If you're hiring a Watson,
get someone who can kick butt.**

MANDRAKE MANDRAKE HAD NEVER DESCENDED into to the dark depths of Gunther Gates Middle School's basement. Above him, a single fluorescent light sputtered, painting the forsaken hallway in its dismal greenish glow. Locker doors dangled from their hinges. Gum and spitballs dotted the ceiling. A torn poster from a bygone era displayed children hiding under their desks as a mushroom cloud exploded outside their window.

But Mandrake's eyes were locked on the far end of the hall — The Detention Dungeon.

He took a deep breath. The gross bleach-y air reminded him of the YMCA change room. The gross stench triggered his gag-reflex. He covered his nostrils with his hand and shuffled across the dusty floor.

In olden times — aka when Grandma was his age — room 016 was the home-economics lab, a place where kids learned to sew and cook and perform other pre-computer-aged tasks needed in the time of dinosaurs and wooden wheels.

These days it served as a place of punishment. Every day, a murderer's row of spitball snipers, homework copiers, and serial wedgiers gathered to pay their after school penance for their crimes.

Mandrake inched inside the classroom, drawing the glare of a dozen hardened tween reprobates.

Again, Mandrake gasped, this time sucking in an unhealthy clump of chalk-polluted air. It settled dry against the back of his throat, and he hacked like a sick cat.

Mandrake always went out of his way to fly under radars. But now here he was, headed into a room with the baddest of the bad.

He was a freak after all, the son of an infamous criminal. Good kids shunned him and the bad kids knew enough to be afraid. His notoriety was like a force-field. In his grade-school days, he made an effort. He tried to join in on their kickball games and schoolyard banter. But whenever he started making headway, a parent would immediately put a stop to any potential BFF scenario. What reasonable adult wanted to invite a kid to a play date, whose father once hijacked every school bus in the city and held them for ransom?

There was an oddball contingent that actually thought it'd be 'wicked cool' to hang out with a villain's son.

Mandrake steered clear of them too. They were a little scary.

Mandrake had zero friends. He justified it with his quest to be a sleuth extraordinaire. No friends meant more time to study and practice the vital skills he needed — burning rope binds with a magnifying glasses, picking the locks of handcuffs, and Morse code burping.

Mandrake surveyed the chair situation. The hodge-podge Civil War-era wooden chair/desk combos were stuffed with back-of-the-bus riffraff. He shuffled past Tyler Tarberry, the eighth-grader who was under investigation for Cherry Bombing the White House bathrooms on a field-trip to D.C. He stepped over the books of Sidney Spence, who once brought a live cobra to show-and-tell. Gloria Riley smiled at him. She had an eye-patch. 'Nuff said.

There was only one seat left, and as fate or destiny would have it — it was next to —

The Ox.

He sat sideways, his bean-bag sized belly too large to squeeze behind the middle-school-sized desk. Blood stains marred his tattered jean jacket. Or pizza sauce. It was Pizza Tuesday in the cafeteria.

Mandrake ducked his head, clutched the straps of his backpack like a parachute, and shuffled over to the empty desk, trying to avoid any direct eye contact. Rules of the jungle and schoolyard recess and all. He spun around and dropped into the seat just as Ox kicked the foot of the desk. The chair launched across the dusty floor and Mandrake's tailbone cannon-balled to the hard concrete floor. Pain jack hammered up his spine.

The gaggle of degenerate Ox-appeasers cackled.

Mandrake wanted to cry, but his survival instincts kicked in. He turned his pain into a bizarre laughter. "Good one, Ox. Well played. I didn't need that spine, anyway." Tears ran down his cheeks. "It'll probably grow back."

Ox stood up and punted Mandrake's backpack across the room.

It hit some poor loser in the face, knocking the kid to the floor and causing a nose bleed. But nobody cared. All eyes were glued to the center ring of this sicko circus.

"I think you're in the wrong place." Ox cracked his knuckles in a way that would make a pediatrician cringe. "This isn't losers club."

Ox's comedy material needed serious work, but the entourage around him snickered anyway. Hecklers ended up with their heads in toilets.

"Ox, this is that Mandrake kid." The voice came from Timmy Daniels. Timmy was Ox's orbit. He was a pimply worm of a kid, and was always circling around, chiming in with a chuckle or a "hit 'em again, Ox", or playing lookout while Ox committed milk-money banditry. "The crook's kid."

Ox's face twitched and his nose twisted up.

Mandrake realized Timmy's warning was no warning at all. It was a dare. Mandrake mentally translated Timmy's words — "Ox, I dare you to beat up the son of the most notorious villain mankind has ever seen."

Ox's chocolate bar stained hands grabbed Mandrake by the collar. He yanked Mandrake to his feet.

"You think your father's all big and bad because he's in prison?"

The suddenness of going from floor to Ox's face made Mandrake's stomach do loop-de-loops. Still he thought it best not to ignore this gargantuan nut job's questions. "No, not at all. Prison's for bad people."

"What?!" Ox lifted Mandrake off his feet. "My dad's in prison. My mom too. My cat's doing hard time in Animal Control. You saying they're bad people?"

Mandrake felt his feet rise from the floor. "No, of course not. I'm sure they're upstanding inmates."

"'Inmates?!' You saying my parents are cousins?" Ox said.

Mandrake choked back an urge to puke. "I think that's inbreeds."

"I'm going to make it my life's mission to show you how bad I really am. I'm going to teach you a lesson about who the real villain of Capital City is." Ox's stink breath floated right up Mandrake's nose. A mix of Pepperoni and never-flossed teeth. Like the stench of a military grade fart.

The smell made Mandrake gag. He looked away trying to stifle his queasiness.

Ox shook him hard. "You got anything to say about, it? Man-FLAKE?"

"Well, I... uh... " And then it happened. Mandrake's stomach snapped like a bear trap. A wave of spew traveled from his gut to his lips before he could finish his sentence.

The yellowish-green vomit splashed Ox in the hair, in the eyes, up his nose, and even into his wide open mouth.

Mandrake immediately regretted his choice of creamed corn as a lunch side.

Ox stood frozen, dripping in the partially digested mix.

The other kids backed up, unable to hide their horror.

And then Ox started to pant. It looked as if he was suppressing tears. Finally, he spit a wad of Mandrake's projectile cream corn and spoke. "YOU. MUST. DIE!"

Ox grabbed Mandrake by the throat. The rabble began to cheer.

Mandrake kicked and screamed as he was once again hoisted off the floor. This kid meant murder. Mandrake kicked and clawed but his desperate life-saving attempts were futile in the hands of Ox's chunky man-haired fists.

Mandrake realized this was his end. His sleuthing career, his attempt to redeem his family, any hope of finding the inspector or bringing down Max Mandrake, all would be snuffed out here, right now.

Skreeeeeeeeeeeech

A ghastly noise stabbed Mandrake's ears and clawed at his soul. Even the enraged Ox cowered, dropping Mandrake and blocking the sound with cupped hands.

Vice Principal Lestrade's yellow fingernails agonizingly scratched across the chalk board at the front of the room.

"Play time is over, degenerates," he said. "Assume the position."

Everyone hurried to the surrounding chalkboard-covered walls and grabbed a piece of chalk. They each had an ample amount of space, giving them plenty of black real estate to work with.

Lestrade approached the Ox. "Ox... go get yourself cleaned up. Be back in five or you're serving double time."

Ox glared at Mandrake through dripping puke, ignoring Lestrade's order.

Lestrade threw an eraser at him. It doinked off his face in a cloud of chalky dust. "Simpkins! Go! Now. And bring a mop back with you to clean up the floor."

Without taking his murderous eyes off Mandrake, Ox slowly

walked out.

Mandrake knew he was in deep trouble. Ox would make him eat an underwear sandwich or drink a bowl of toilet water or wedgie him from the Capital City Clock Tower.

Mandrake's dread was interrupted by Lestrade's authoritative voice. "I talked to Mr. Tinkletot. The grades on yesterday's vocabulary quiz were atrociously poor. So we're gonna do the exact same words again today."

"But we've been doing these for the last two weeks," Timmy whined.

"You should have thought about that before you put super glue on all the staff bathroom toilet seats." Lestrade moved on.

Lestrade handed out each detentionee a sheet of paper which listed ten vocabulary words and their definitions.

Mandrake recognized them immediately. They were the exact word/definition pairs scrawled in colorful graffiti all over Lestrade's car. That's it! The vandalism was payback. Whoever perpetrated the crime was here.

The most likely suspect, of course, was the Ox.

"Totally worth it," Timmy muttered under his breath.

Lestrade clapped his hands. "Okay... give me fifty. No mistakes. Go!"

Like runners taking off at a starter pistol, the delinquents jumped to writing, filling the room with the furious squeaking of chalk as they hurriedly copied the ten vocabulary words from the list on the piece of paper.

But not Mandrake. His mind swam with visions of the hideously gum-prominent smile he'd be sporting after Ox extracted his teeth via knuckle-sandwich.

Even if he managed to survive this afternoon, he was now forever on Ox's list. Mandrake couldn't outmatch the brute in a schoolyard brawl. Perhaps Lestrade could enroll him in a Bullied Protection Program that would give him new fingerprints, and a new family, and inject him with an animal hair goatee, rendering him unrecognizable and unfindable.

Lestrade casually strolled toward Mandrake. "Everything okay, Mr. Mandrake?"

"The Ox... is going to dismember me."

"Don't worry about Ox. If you don't figure out who desecrated my car in the next hour, you're gonna have to deal with your Grandma." Lestrade's eyes shifted to the other kids, who were starting to take notice. "People are staring. Now get to writing before you blow your cover."

He was right. Mandrake was supposed to be here serving detention. He needed to play the part. He raised his chalk as high as he could and began copying the words from his paper:

Surreptitious - (adjective) Stealthy, furtive, secretive

Mandrake took a surreptitious survey of the room. Around him the other detentionees scrawled the words at an impossible speed, filling the boards with words.

Lestrade paced behind them, watching, ready to pounce on a single spelling or typographical error. If he saw one, he'd erase the board, forcing the writer to start from scratch all over again.

Ox returned, wiping his wet hands on his jeans, and took the spot next to Mandrake.

Mandrake smiled apologetically.

Ox bit into a piece of chalk and glared. Crunch, crunch, crunch.

Ox picked up a piece and went to work. He didn't even have to look at the board or the paper, preferring to keep his primal eyes locked on Mandrake. He'd done this so many times, he could write out every definition and word from memory.

Mandrake squealed and returned his attention to the task at hand.

He needed to hurry. He needed to finish his work before Ox, otherwise, the bully and his cronies would be waiting outside for him, ready to spring a trap.

Epitaph - An inscription, generally on a tomb, that serves as a memorial to the deceased.

Mandrake gulped... if he didn't hurry... they'd be authoring his.

He read the next word.

Finesse

He wrote the word. F-I-N-E-S-E.

As he wrote it, Lestrade shoved him aside. "It's Finesse! Two S's! Start over!" Lestrade erased all of Mandrake's writing. "Again!"

He glanced at Ox. The oversized man-child was already three words past 'finesse' and speeding toward a quick finish.

"TIMEOUT!" Mandrake shouted.

Everyone stopped what they were doing.

"MR. MANDRAKE!" Vice Principal Lestrade's spit flung from his lips. "There's no timeout in detention." Lestrade stepped close and whispered, "Do you have my proof?"

"Not yet. But I have an idea." Mandrake coughed. He clutched his stomach and wheezed. His tongue hung out as he spun in circles, finally crashing against the chalkboard.

"What's wrong with you?" Lestrade said. "Should I call an exorcist?"

"It's my asthma. Probably the chalk. Can I go to my locker and get my Gaspirator?" Mandrake winked theatrically.

"I think you mean aspirator," Lestrade said. "Why are you winking at me?"

"It's a symptom!" Mandrake lied. "I can prove it to you. I can prove everything. But I need to leave now."

Lestrade checked his watch. "You have ten minutes. Then it's over."

Ox slashed a finger across his throat and mimed the word "over."

"How come he gets a timeout?" Timmy whined.

Lestrade again erased all of Timmy's work. "Anybody else want a timeout?"

Everyone resumed writing.

"Ten minutes," Lestrade pointed to his watch.

Mandrake grabbed his backpack and sprinted out into the hall. He dug out his phone and set a timer for "10:00 minutes"

He could do this. He'd had five minutes to figure out the Bearded Bank Bandit and only needed four.

But the stakes were personally higher this time. Ox was a psycho. And Crash wasn't here to handle the rough parts.

Mandrake brought up the phone picture of the Vice Principal's graffiti-vandalized sports car. He enlarged a section on the front hood, specifically the word 'finesse'. It was misspelled. Only a single 's'.

Ox could spell out the entire sheet without looking. There's no way he'd screw up that word.

He wasn't the vandalist. Neither were any of the kids in that room. And what to make of the signature — "OX OX OX OX"?

This was a frame job.

But who? So many students feared Ox.

Who had the courage, the guile, the lack of morals, the motive?

Mandrake had eight minutes and forty seconds to figure it out. He'd better hurry.

Amateur Sleuth Rule #20

Fashion tip: Long trench coats are hard to run in. Instead, invest in a good pair of sneakers.

WITH SEVEN-MINUTES TO SAVE his life, Mandrake reached the second floor of Gunther Gates Middle School. The school's halls were like a ghost town at this time of day. A pop quiz tumbleweed rolled in the windy breeze of an air-conditioning unit.

He had free rein. But for what? Where to start?

The entire student body feared Ox. Even his so-called friends had been bullied by the evil oaf at one time or another.

He needed to narrow the suspects. He was looking for a kid who couldn't spell finesse.

Mandrake hurried to Mr. Tinkletot's classroom and raced to the large wooden teacher's desk.

He checked his cellphone alarm — six minutes and twenty seconds left.

Mandrake ripped open the desk's top drawer, revealing a bounty of confiscated cellphones, love notes, paper airplanes, and even a caricature soap-sculpture of Vice Principal Lestrade.

He then moved to the middle drawer. There he found a cache of pill bottles, stress balls and back massagers.

The bottom drawer was stuffed with stacks of tests, homework, and pop-quizzes.

Mandrake shuffled through them, tearing past chunks of ungraded assignments, worksheets, and quizzes.

His fingers stopped on a file labeled "VOCABULARY HOMEWORK."

The thicket of papers was dated last Wednesday. The assignment was to use the ten words in a sentence. All the words were there — Epitaph, Surreptitious and Finesse. This paper, Molly Sanderson's, was perfect. An A+. She was innocent.

Mandrake hurried through the rest, honing in on the in-question word. Surprisingly, most of them nailed the two S's. About halfway through, with only five minutes left, Mandrake found one that didn't. He zeroed in on the sentence:

"My teacher asked me to use finese in the form of a sentence."

Only one 's'. At the top of the page was the signed name of his prime suspect — "Billy Doocy".

Mandrake knew Billy. Everyone did. He headed up the school's A/V Club. In fact, he was its sole member. Whenever there was a TV or slide projector needed for class, the scrawny boy with the bug-eyes would set it up. He had horrible posture, a weird overbite, and was prime bully-bait.

Mandrake crept toward Principal Baldacci's office. He'd passed the office enough times to know that a huge chart hung on Baldacci's wall behind her desk. The chart cataloged student locker assignments. Mandrake needed to find the location of Billy's locker to search it for evidence.

His phone alarm had ticked down to four minutes.

Mandrake burst into the office. Six PTA types stared back at him, along with Principal Baldacci.

"Mandrake Mandrake?" Baldacci stood. "Why are you here?"

Mandrake spied the wall chart, but the writing was too small to read without careful study. "Uh... to see you."

"We're in the middle of a very important meeting. You'll have to wait outside till we're done." Baldacci checked her watch. "Say ten minutes."

"No," Mandrake said. "I can't wait that long. I... uh... need a selfie."

"A selfie?" Baldacci asked.

"Yeah, it's for the... uh... world's best principal contest," Mandrake riffed. "It was supposed to be a surprise."

"Well, this is very flattering, but I'm sure it can wait."

"No!" Mandrake shouted. "The deadline is in five minutes. I'd kick myself if someone else won the free cruise around the world besides the actual best principal ever. "

Baldacci blushed. "Okay, just hurry it up."

Mandrake threw one arm around Baldacci and stretched his other arm out, framing them in a selfie. His actual focus was on the large wall chart just to the right of the principal's head.

"Shouldn't my face be in the picture?" Baldacci said.

"Probably," Mandrake pressed the button, perfectly capturing Baldacci's shoulder and the locker diagram. "Okay, gotta run."

"Let me know if I win," Baldacci called after him.

"I wouldn't get your hopes up." Mandrake dashed back into the hall.

Mandrake pinch zoomed in on the photo. He scanned the locker assignments, finding the one labeled "B. Doocy."

Locker 177!

He sprinted off, checking the time. One minute and fifty-four seconds. .

Mandrake slid to a stop in front of the locker and pulled his heavy American History Book from his backpack. The book had been hollowed out and hidden inside was a small-sized Allen wrench, a screwdriver, and a set of lock-picks.

Mandrake had gotten pretty good at picking locks around the house, but he'd never field-tested his skill. He lifted the combination lock, exposing the small keyhole in the back. All padlocks had master keys in case students forgot their combination. But these keyholes left them vulnerable.

Mandrake stuck the pick inside.

"Hey!" came a shout from the locker.

Mandrake jumped back. The locker was alive! It talked.

"Who's there?" The voice questioned from inside the locker. A boy's voice. It cracked in fear. "Ox? I swear. I didn't know you were allergic to vegetables. My mother packed that sandwich. I promise if you give me the chance, I'll make it up to you. I'll make have her pack donuts or cheeseburgers or Ice Cream or whatever you want."

Mandrake leaned in close and whispered, "It's not Ox. It's Mandrake Mandrake."

"Mandrake?! You gotta help me. Ox locked me in here because he didn't like the lunch he stole from me. He's coming back for me after detention. I only have a few minutes." The locker door began to rattle.

Mandrake checked his timer. One minute and ten seconds to go.

"Let me out! My combination is —!"

Mandrake slammed a fist against the locker. "Don't tell me. I can pick it." Mandrake went back to the lock. "You're not claustrophobic are you?"

"No. Just Ox-o-phobic!"

"So, you framed Ox? You spray painted the Vice Principal's car."

"I don't know what you're talking about." The pitch of Billy's voice rose.

Mandrake eased back. "Oh, well, I better get going then."

"Wait! You can't just leave me here."

"I have a mystery to solve," Mandrake said. "And if you don't want to help me, why should I help you?"

"Well, because you're a decent human being? And if you leave me here, Ox will make me eat a sock taco."

Mandrake rocked back on his heels. He knew what it was like to be on Ox's death-list. He wanted to help the kid, but he needed to help himself first. "Good luck, Billy. It's been nice knowing you... "

"Okay! Fine. I spray-painted Vice Principal Lestrade's car. Okay? But please don't tell anybody. Do you know what Ox would do to me if he found out I tried to frame him?"

"I have a pretty good idea. But I have to tell Lestrade. I don't have a choice."

"Do what you gotta do." Billy paused. "Whatever. Maybe I'll get lucky and he'll expel me! Then I won't have to spend another day sharing a homeroom with that monster."

Mandrake sighed. He felt for the kid. Billy didn't deserve to be expelled any more than he deserved to be trapped in this locker. "Maybe there's another way... to take care of both of our problems. But I need that can of paint."

"Thirty-forty-twenty-five," Billy replied immediately.

Mandrake sighed. He spun the numbers and opened the lock. The door swung open and a tidal wave of books flooded out and crashed at Mandrake's feet.

Inside the locker, Billy gasped for air and cried tear of joy, his limbs pretzeled around his body.

"My spine is forever in your debt." Contorting his shoulder, Billy handed over the offending spray-paint can.

Mandrake grabbed a handful of the books piled at his feet. They weren't textbooks. Instead they had curious titles like CARD TRICKS TO PICK UP CHICKS, HOUDINI'S SECRETS REVEALED and CONFESSIONS OF A BALLOON ANIMAL ARTIST.

"Hey!" Billy cried. "Those are for magician's eyes only!"

Suddenly, the phone alarm blared. Mandrake dropped the books. His head whipped around, checking both ends of the hallway.

"What?! What's wrong?" Billy leaned forward.

Mandrake slammed the locker shut on the boy's face.

"Hey! I thought we had a deal."

"Ox is coming. You're safer in there. And I need your help with something else. Just keep quiet... I'll be back for you." Mandrake dashed off.

He had one shot at surviving this.

Twenty-One

Amateur Rule #21: Fashion tip: Black belt NO. Bulletproof vest YES.

Five minutes past Lestrade's imposed deadline, Mandrake raced into the Detention Dungeon.

Vocabulary words screamed back at him from the blackboards. But their degenerate authors were nowhere to be found. Neither was Lestrade.

Somewhere in these grimy halls lurked a bully with a vendetta.

He needed to get to Lestrade first. Mandrake pulled out his phone and searched his contact info.

A ham-handed fist grabbed Mandrake by the back of his shirt and yanked him into the hall. He crashed into the old lockers, leaving a middle-schooler-sized dent.

Ox and his gang surrounded Mandrake.

"Ox." Mandrake forced a laugh, sounding a tad crazy. "I was just looking for you. I wanted to apologize"

"Too late for that." Ox balled his fist and sucked in his blubbery belly, redistributing the girth to his chest. "It's payback time!"

Ox hoisted Mandrake and wedged him inside an open locker.

Mandrake began to sweat. He wasn't claustrophobic, but being locked down here was similar to being buried alive. "Wait. You can't just lock me inside!"

"Oh... we're not just gonna lock you inside." A sinister grin stretched across Ox's face.

Ox's scrawny minion, Timmy, dumped out the bully's overstuffed backpack, spilling dozens of stolen paper bag lunches onto the grime covered floor.

Ox scooped up an armful of paper bags and began stuffing his face. Oreos, sliced bananas, chips, cheese sandwiches, all down the hatch. He tore open yogurt and rice pudding cups and ketch-up packets and squeezed them down his throat.

"Here's my plan," he mumbled through his gopher cheeks of lunchables. "I'm eating all of these lunches. Then I'm going to bathe you in blown chunks and lock you inside this locker. So you can stew in spew."

"And I'm going to record it." Timmy held up his cell phone. "For prosperity."

Ox punched him in the arm. "Speak American."

"My bad." Timmy rubbed his shoulder and slid behind Ox's other minions. "For... fun?"

Mandrake pleaded. He wanted to kneel but the tight confines of the locker restricted his movements. "Ox! You can't do this —"

"You threw-up in my mouth, Man-dork. Puke for a puke!" With the p-sounds, tuna-sandwich bits sprayed from his mouth onto Mandrake's glasses. "Like it says in the Bible."

"I don't think it actually —"

Ox stopped, grabbed Mandrake's shirt, and twisted it, drawing him up inches away from his lunch-compactor mouth. "You calling me a heathen?"

"The Bible is open to many interpretations."

Ox slammed Mandrake against the back of the locker and resumed shoving fist-fulls of bologna into his clogged food hole. His eyes drooped, his skin yellowed. He looked dizzy as he held his gut and massaged his blubber.

"Line me up!" Ox said.

The Ox-ettes peeled open forty school issued milk cartons.

Oh-no. Mandrake had seen the viral videos where foolish kids were tricked into attempting to drink a gallon of milk in one sitting, a sucker bet that always ended in a grand finale of regurgitation. Ox's line of pints probably added up to three times that much.

He chugged away. Milk spilled down the side of his face and soaked his beard. One after another he guzzled, crushed the carton, and chucked it away. Regular milk, chocolate, and strawberry poured past Ox's crooked teeth and sloshed down his throat. Until finally, he lifted up the last carton — skim… and drank half of it.

He'd reached some biological limit. A deep inhuman rumble emitted from his gut. "Okay stomach!" Ox pushed and prodded at his belly. "Bring the spew."

"OXYMANDIAS SIMPKINS!" A voice boomed through the hall.

Lestrade stood right behind him.

Ox turned, trying to hold the eruption that simmered like a Witch's Cauldron inside his stomach.

Lestrade's red face scanned the clutter of wrappers, napkins, apple cores and banana peels that littered the floor. "What is going on here?"

Ox clamped his lips tight and shook his head. Tears pooled in his bulging eyes.

"Nothing to say for yourself?" Lestrade scowled. "Doesn't matter. Cause I got you. I finally got you. We found this inside your locker. "

Lestrade raised something from behind his back — a history book. "An anonymous tip."

Mandrake gave a sly smile.

Lestrade opened the book. Inside the center was carved out — this was Mandrake's special book!

But instead of lock-picking tools, the offending spray-paint can was centered in the middle.

Ox threw a hand over his mouth and shook his head.

"It was in your locker. And unless some lock pick expert broke in and hid a spray-paint can inside, I'd say you have some explaining to do," Lestrade sneered. "What? Cat got your tongue? Do you have nothing to say?"

Ox opened his mouth and a fountain of chunky vomit hydranted out. The hurl blasted Lestrade's face, knocking his glasses off, flooding his nostrils and eyes, polluting his hair, and filling his breast pocket.

The second wave was worse than the first. A geyser of liquefied treats and fruit and milk shot forth.

Lestrade didn't blink. He didn't even pick off the bits of corn and raisin that littered his bile soaked skin. "Oxymandias, to my office! NOW!"

Ox hurried off. His minions scattered.

Lestrade whispered back to Mandrake. "Mr. Mandrake, it seems I owe you one."

Then he squished off.

AMATEUR SLEUTH RULE #22

Only crooks and villains use the word 'preposterous.'

MANDRAKE YANKED OPEN THE LOCKER door. Billy Doocy spilled out and crashed face-first on the floor.

Mandrake pulled the boy to his feet. "Are you okay?"

"Spleen fell asleep. Not the first time. I've spent half my middle-school career trapped lockers. Like a second home." Billy hammered his right fist into his back. "Just got to wake it up. Spleens will be the least of our problem if we're still here when The Ox comes back."

"The Ox isn't coming back," Mandrake said. "I took care of him."

"You took care of him?" Billy slashed a finger across his throat. "Did you get your father to do the deed?"

"No!" Mandrake shouted. "I just finished the job you started. With the spray paint."

"Death by spray-paint?!"

"No. Expelled because of spray-paint."

"Expelled!" Billy fell to his knees and hugged Mandrake's ankles and kissed his tennis shoes. "How can I ever thank you?"

"You can start by not doing that." Mandrake pulled his feet away. "And there's something else."

Mandrake reached in his backpack and pulled out the Betamax video.

Moments later, the two huddled in the back of the AV closet, behind dust-covered film cans, broken projectors and never-used slide machines. Billy ran colored wires from a clunky old black box to a sturdy television 50 years past its prime.

"I haven't seen one of these since the great video wars of the 1980's." Billy said, referring to the video.

"You weren't born in the 1980s." Mandrake folded his arms.

"If you don't know your history, you're doomed to repeat it." Billy punched the video machine's power button. "Betamax was actually a better format, but VHS had more marketing know-how. Sometimes, it's not about being better. It's about being in the headlines." Billy pressed the eject button on the Betamax machine and the lid on the top mechanically popped open, leaving enough space to insert Mandrake's tape. "This might eat your tape."

"The machine has teeth?" Mandrake peered inside.

"In my line of business, it's best to assume the worst." Billy pushed the tape into the mouth of the thing and flipped a switch on the television.

The TV glowed as the Betamax's gears growled.

"So, what are we watching? Home movies? Tell me it's not a birthing video. My parents showed me my delivery on my last birthday." Billy shuddered. "Now, I get woozy whenever my mom does Yoga."

A blurry black-and-white image of Max Mandrake's prison cell filled the screen. Max stood near his bed, finger-painting on a canvas.

Billy whacked the TV with an open palm, sending a spike of static through the feed. "That's an A/V Club trick by the way. Should only be attempted by trained professionals."

It seemed to help.

"This is the time code." Billy pointed to the digits that ticked away in the bottom right-hand corner of the screen. "That's military time. What a joke. A conspiracy to sell more watches."

Mandrake mentally converted the number "1915:01" to 7:15pm. Less than an hour from when Crash Brickfist came knocking on Mandrake's front door that evening.

"I'm not sure about this other code." Billy pointed. "Probably a location designation."

"It's Max Mandrake's prisoner number," Mandrake said.

"Whoa!' Billy's jaw dropped. "That's him? Mr. Evil Incarnate. The biggest of bads. The man who beat out Attila the Hun and Vlad the Impaler in the Most Hated Man Ever contest? I mean... I know he's your dad. I'm sure he plays catch in the backyard and helps you build forts and cheat at the science fair. But still."

"Billy, this is private," Mandrake said.

"Of course. I won't tell anyone," Billy replied. "Would you have to kill me if I did?"

Mandrake clenched his fists and pushed his lips together, trying to hold back the words his raging brain demanded he say. This kid was annoying.

The TV's cheap speakers rumbled. On screen, the cell's bulletproof glass wall opened. Max turned, wiping his fingers on some tissues.

The Inspector stepped into the cell. For a moment, the two stared at one another like gunslingers at high-noon.

"Inspector Gates, have you come to apologize for arresting me?" Max sat at the small table and invited the Inspector to sit across from him.

Inspector Gates turned to face the screen, as if he was looking right at Mandrake. "Warden, please take us off sound. In the interest of the security of Capital City this audio is not to be recorded."

Billy reached down to the box and hit a pause button. The image froze. A bar of static cut through the middle. "I know this old guy. He's a cop or something. Right?"

"There's a statue of him out front," Mandrake said, not taking his eyes off the screen. "Our school is named after him. Gunther Gates Middle.

"Ooooh. I thought he was Einstein or some old president or

spelling bee champion. I thought statues were only of dead guys. Isn't that a law or something?"

Mandrake willed his eyes not to roll as he hit the play button.

The video continued. A heated conversation ensued between the Inspector and Max. The words could not be heard, only the droning hum of white noise.

After a few moments of yelling and finger pointing, the Inspector placed his large metal suitcase on the table.

Billy paused the tape again. "Nothing's gonna jump out of the suitcase, is it? I'm not good with the jump scares. Weak bladder. My pediatrician diagnosed it."

Mandrake ignored him. The Inspector perched his thumbs against the suitcase's bronzed double-clasps. In unison, he pressed down.

Suddenly, the black and white image went dark. Not a sliver of light marked the screen. Only the rolling superimposed time code remained visible.

"Whoa. A power failure?" Billy stuck his face inches from the TV. "This is getting good. I mean, I'm not sure it's 'pay to watch it in Imax' good, but I'd give it a watch on basic cable."

The lights returned. The Inspector's fingers were still perched on the buttons of his suitcase.

But Max Mandrake was gone. There was no sign of him anywhere. Nowhere to hide. He'd just vanished.

"What the frig?! He's a warlock." Billy held his phone up, capturing video of the screen.

"Hey!" Mandrake blocked the TV. "You've been recording this?"

"How am I supposed to help analyze it, if I don't have a copy?" Billy stood on a chair to get a clear shot over Mandrake.

"You're not!" Mandrake jumped for the phone but couldn't quite reach. "Delete that video!"

On screen, the Inspector shuffled along the perimeter of the cell, prodding the walls with his hands and fingers.

Billy jumped off the chair as Mandrake chased him around. "I bet he's got a cloaking device? Or an invisibility ring?" Billy prattled on. "Or maybe aliens teleported him out of the prison and are probing him on their spaceship."

The Inspector turned and stared directly up at the camera. He clenched his left-eye shut and opened his right monocled eye wide.

Mandrake stared right back at him. The hairs on his arms standing straight, his skin tingled. "That's it!"

"Max Mandrake has escaped! We're all in danger," Billy cried. "We should warn someone! Get home. Lock our doors. Hide our comic-book collections!"

The scene continued to unfold on the television. The glass entrance of the cell opened. The Inspector grabbed the suitcase and stormed out.

Mandrake barely paid attention. His mind racing — the face, the eye, the monocle. The right eye.

"If you leave the tape with me, I could run some tests."

Mandrake grabbed the entire Betamax player and yanked the cords from their connection. "No!"

"You can't just take that," Billy protested. "That's school property."

"Well, you can't just go spray paint a Vice Principal's sports car," Mandrake replied. "So if you don't want to end up back in that locker, you'll talk to no one about this. And delete that video!"

Mandrake tucked the Betamax player under his arm and hurried down the main steps and raced to the courtyard near the bus lane. He stopped at the bronze statue of Inspector Gates, its sculpted face staring down at Sally, his signature silver time-piece. The monument appeared identical to the real life version Mandrake had just watched on screen — stern, just, serious, maybe even constipated. The monocle set in his left eye.

Mandrake grinned. Whoever walked out of the prison the other night wore the monocle in their right eye!

It was Max! He didn't disappear. He walked right out of the inescapable prison, dressed as the Inspector himself.

Mandrake's jack hammered. This was huge! He could taste the headlines proclaiming how he, a mere boy, solved a mystery that stumped even the world's greatest detectives. He was claiming this victory for himself.

Other questions lingered. Where did he get the disguise? What happened to the Inspector? And most importantly, where was Max Mandrake right now?

Right now, none of that mattered. It was time to cash in. He tucked the VCR beneath his arm and skipped off.

HOOOOOOOOOOOOONK!!! The blaring horn blasted Mandrake's eardrums and caused him to shriek in surprise. He rubbed his ears and sucked in a calming breath, filling his head with gas fumes. He coughed and gagged as he recognized the noxious stench of Crash Brickfist's supercharger.

Amateur Sleuth Rule #23

If it starts getting personal, you may be missing clues.

Crash poked his head out of the supercharger's driver's side window. "Get in."

"Ah, no thanks," Mandrake said. Over a mile and a half laid before him on his long walk home, but he refused to undergo a Crash Brickfist passenger-seat shakedown. "I need the walk. Trying to break in a new pair of sneaks."

Crash's eyes shifted to the cumbersome video player wedged uncomfortably in Mandrake's armpit. "What's today? Throwback Thursday?"

"Class project." Mandrake squirmed. "History of audio visual devices."

Crash growled.

"Gotta run. I have a lot of rewinding ahead of me." Mandrake shuffled off, escaping Crash's clam-eyed gaze.

Crash's supercharger lurched up the curb and blocked Mandrake's path. "We found the Inspector."

Mandrake laughed. He cackled, even.

"What's going on with you?" Crash frowned.

"Nothing." Mandrake felt beads of perspiration wetting his forehead. He hated lying but he was done with other people stealing his rightful kudos. The Age of Mandrake was about to begin!!

HONK! Crash pumped the horn. "Come on. We're on the clock."

"I've got homework. And curfew. Besides, if the Inspector is back," Mandrake stifled another laugh, "Why would you need me? A mere boy? I'm sure the good old Inspector knows exactly where to find Max."

"You're one of The Seven.

"I quit The Seven."

"I heard. I'll get you back in."

"I don't want back in. Those people didn't want me in the first place. And I don't need them." Mandrake walked around the car's bumper but Crash edged the Supercharger forward.

"It's not safe until we figure this out," Crash grumbled.

"We? Don't you mean 'I'?" Mandrake snorted. It actually took him by surprise. He was a snorter now?

Crash revved his engine. "Kid, come on —"

"No Crash! I'm done solving cases so you can take all the credit."

Crash shut off the growling engine and fixed Mandrake with a stare. "You wanna know why your father quit The Seven? He was sick of Inspector Gates getting all the credit for his hard work. He wanted the accolades. The glory."

Mandrake's fists balled. "You get paid for what you do. You get medals, keys to the city, your name in the paper. What makes you the good guy?"

"Maybe it's cause I'd do it even if nobody cared."

Mandrake balled his toes inside his sneakers. Enough was enough. Mandrake had been cracking cases for the greater good for almost two years now – when was the last time Crash did something just because? When was the last time Mandrake's heroics were splashed all over the front-page of the news?!!

"Come on, kid," Crash pleaded. "You know I've been your biggest fan."

"Are you?" Mandrake crossed his arms. "Why did you really take me with you, the night we caught the Bearded Bank Bandit? Was it just about the case, or something else?"

"Kid, let's not do this —-"

"That night, when I was in the closet, what did you tell my grandmother?"

Crash scowled. He looked down at Mandrake's shoes. Mandrake had never known Crash to be afraid to lock eyes with anyone.

"I suppose it's on a 'need to know' basis?" Mandrake's shoulders sagged.

"Kid, I believe in you. I do. But I also want you to be safe."

"Well, I can fend for myself." Mandrake hopped on top of Crash's car and slid across the windshield —

-        but his shirt caught on the wiper and he stuck there.

Crash lowered the passenger window. "You need to tell me if you've got anything on the case."

Mandrake ripped his shirt and fell off the car. "When I do, you'll read about it in the papers. Like everyone else."

Mandrake marched home.

Tonight would be the start of the Age of Mandrake!

Amateur Sleuth Rule #24

**Villains are in it for the money.
Supervillains are in it for the fame.**

THE WORLD'S GREATEST DETECTIVE SET upon an impossible mystery — how to tie a necktie! Mandrake knew knots. He studied how to escape a Singapore Sheep Shank and the dreaded KGB half hitch. But the standard Windsor was harder than a decade old cold-case with no DNA evidence and zero eyewitnesses. Instead of a father or an uncle to teach him the ways of boy-dom, the Internet often served as Mandrake's surrogate father. Past searches educated him in hocking loogies, belching the Star-Spangled Banner, and even peeing standing up.

Mandrake didn't dare let Grandma in on his scheme. She'd likely ship him off to boarding school. In Antarctica.

Mandrake's plan was simple. He'd sneak out the back door, march right into WCAP Studios and plunk down the Betamax VCR. He'd show ace anchor Giles Geronimo and his audience the startling prison escape video and talk them through the erroneous monocle placement, reassuring everyone he was on the case.

The station would interrupt whatever sitcom or cop-drama to break the news. It would be a great public introduction to the newest hot-shot detective in town. If there was time, he'd even clue them in on how he — not Crash Brickfist — brought down the Bearded Bank Bandit.

The only thing standing in his way was this stupid tie.

He looped the long side over the smaller twice, then pulled the business end through the jumble in the middle and yanked it taut.

Ta-da! The perfect Windsor knot. Perfect, except for his right hand which was trapped inside its center. He tried to wriggle his hand out but the force tightened its grip, erasing any and all slack. His fingers tingled from the choked-off circulation. He tugged, pulling his neck down like the ceremonial bow before a Karate tournament.

Slam! The door downstairs smashed open. A loud shatter! Glass breaking!

Grandma?! Was she okay?! Did Max Mandrake come to finish him off before he could publicly spoil his magical escape?

He stepped toward the door, then stopped. How would he manage hand-to-hand combat with his dominate hand bound tightly to his throat?

Outside, an engine growled, tires squealed, and metal scraped concrete.

Mandrake rushed to the window, just in time to see Grandma's car rumble down the driveway and round the street corner.

Where she was going? It wasn't Bridge Night or Bingo.

He raced down the stairs. She'd left the front door wide open. Beside her chair lay an abandoned spoon full of Tapioca pudding. Her shoes sat parked by the door. Her coat hung from its hanger.

Mandrake could hear the droning voice of the TV news anchor.

"Video surveillance has confirmed — Max Mandrake has escaped!"

A live news report played. Mandrake read the scrolling text at the bottom of the screen: "Max Mandrake breaks out of maximum security prison! Video surveillance confirms the escape!"

Prison video? Mandrake thought to himself. My prison video?

On screen, the pint-sized freckled face audio-visual club informant, Billy Doocy, stood before a forest of microphones. He was dressed in his Sunday best, complete with a perfectly knotted tie. He held up his phone. "I can't say where I got the footage. But as president of Gunther Gates Middle School's A.V. Club, I can assure you it's legit."

Mandrake dropped to his knees. His jaw fell slack. Billy Doocy was stealing his moment! His glory!

Billy dropped his voice down an octave for gravitas. "The video is chilling. In my line of work I see a lot of raw footage. PG-13 even. Please, if you have young children or small pets around... you might want to turn the channel."

Billy hit play on his phone. An AV club projector displayed his recording of the prison security video on a large stand-up screen positioned at the foot of the Inspector Statue at the stairs of the middle school entrance.

The overhead shot of Max Mandrake's prison played out. Billy poked his head in front of the cameras and positioned himself for a close-up. "We may be dealing with a warlock."

"AAAAAAAAAAH!" Mandrake kung-fu kicked the television, knocking it backward. Its power cord ripped from the outlet causing the picture to snap off."This was my moment!" He stomped on the face of the fallen TV. "Mine! Mine! MINE!!!!"

Mandrake demanded justice! This clip-on-wearing con artist needed to be exposed as a fraud!

Mandrake marched out to front door. Nothing could stop the Age of Mandrake! Nothing!

Except for the five cops standing on his porch with their guns aimed at his face.

"Hands in the air!!" The white-haired cop with the gizzard neck cried.

"I can't." Mandrake nodded at his hand bound by neck wear. He wiggled his tingling fingers to call attention to it.

The geezer cop pinched his lapel radio. "This is Captain Lloyd. We've got an injured kid. His hand's in a sling. Or a tourniquet. Or a sling-o-quet? Over."

"It's not a sling. It's a knot."

The cop went back to the walkie. "Negative on the sling-o-quet. The kid's been tied up! Over." He turned to his team. "Surround the house. Max Mandrake must be here."

The squad of cops spread out, inching their way toward the sides of the house, sticking tight to the powder blue aluminum siding while trampling Grandma's Azaleas.

"No!" Mandrake protested. "This isn't a kidnapping, it's a wardrobe malfunction."

The captain sized him up. "I'm no fashionista but typically, the hand goes on the outside."

Mandrake rolled his eyes. "I don't have time for this! I need to get to the middle school! Max Mandrake has escaped!"

"Ah, yeah, we all saw the video. That Doocy kid's going to be a celebrity." The captain guided Mandrake toward his police cruiser parked at the curb. "They're talking book deals. Reality shows. Mayor wants to give him a key to the city."

"You can't give a key to a thief!" Mandrake turned to run.

"Whoa there, lefty!" The captain grabbed Mandrake by the shoulder and ushered him toward the backseat. "We've been ordered to put you on lock-down."

"Lock-down?" Mandrake scrunched his forehead. "By who?"

"Crash Brickfist."

Mandrake stomped his foot. "Bah!"

The captain pushed his cap to the side to scratch his head. "Is that supposed to be a sheep impersonation?"

"No, it's an exclamation. It means 'ridiculous'."

The captain frowned. "Maybe to a sheep."

Mandrake shook his head. "Brickfist doesn't work for the police. He has no authority."

"Authority? Have you seen his fists? They're like boulders with knuckles. I just got dental work." The officer flashed a perfect smile. "I can't risk my new caps."

"Your teeth and everyone's teeth are in jeopardy!"

"You mean... Gingivitis?"

Mandrake sighed. "I have vital information."

The captain ushered Mandrake inside the back of the cruiser. "Well, it's going to have to wait till we get you to the station." He shut the door and climbed in the front.

BZZZ-AAT. The police radio belched a stream of static, followed by a tin voice. "All units. Code Munchkin. Repeat Code Munchkin. All air traffic to and from Crime Island Prison needs to be cleared by order of Inspector Gunther Gates! Only his helicopter is allowed in the sky."

"The Inspector isn't the Inspector! He's sending in the Sleuthing Seven!" Mandrake leaned forward. "It's a trick."

"Let the grownups do the crime fighting, kid." The Captain started the car.

The grown-ups?! Mandrake's blood boiled. "Give me the radio! I need to call the Sleuthing Seven!!"

Mandrake reached over the seat and grabbed the microphone. The Captain ripped it away, snapping it off the base.

"Enough!" The Captain stared at the broken radio. "You broke my radio! What do you have to say for yourself?"

"Um... " Mandrake pointed at the house. "There! It's Max Mandrake!"

The Captain charged out and pulled his gun. "Where?"

"Second floor. In my room! He's disguised as a stuffed elephant."

The Captain rushed out and ducked behind a tree. He barked orders to the other cops. "Get the elephant, dead or alive."

They busted into the house.

They wouldn't find anything. Mandrake had lied. Lying to the cops wasn't a thing he took likely. But it was small potatoes compared to what he was about to do — Grand Theft Police Car!

Amateur Sleuth Rule #25

A good detective doesn't play by the rules!

DRIVING A CAR WASN'T HARD, but reaching the pedals while trying to see over the dashboard was impossible.

Mandrake had a strategy. He stomped on the gas, then popped up, steered wildly, and laid on the horn. Pedestrians and cars scattered in front of him.

Mandrake's technique wasn't perfect, as both the screaming jogger on Parkway Drive and the soda-can throwing hot dog stand owner on Madison could attest. Luckily, the flashing lights and blaring siren warned off most of the human speed bumps in his path.

Unsure how to stop, Mandrake barreled over the Baker Street Library's curb and smashed into one of the bronze bloodhound statues that stood guard out front. The two-ton sculpted dog timbered toward him. SMAAAAAAASH! Its snout punched through the thick windshield, shattering the glass. The marble hound's dead eyes glared directly into Mandrake's saucer-eyed gaze.

"Not bad for a first time." The boy detective shook off window shards and unhooked his seat belt. "No deaths. That's a win."

He hopped out of the car, swung his backpack over his shoulder and trotted up the steep stairs to the library's double-doors.

DINK-DINK-DINK. His delicate fist pounded the sturdy wood.

"Let me in!" Mandrake yelled. "You can't go to Crime Island! It's a trap! It's a —"

His cries were interrupted by an incredible rush of noise and air. The rocket chopper shot off the roof. Air blasted the ground, kicking up dirt and mussing Mandrake's hair, tornado-style. The rotors thundered in his ears forcing him to squeeze the sides of his head as the flying machine soared off over the city.

"Stop! No!" Mandrake shouted and waved his arms skyward.

The chopper roared off, rattling a church steeple and a movie billboard in its wake. No doubt, The Seven were packed inside, eyes locked on the inescapable prison, readying for battle.

They were doomed.

Behind him, a metallic twang rang out like two aluminum baseball bats being cymbal smashed together.

The doors had unlocked. The heavy wooden doubles parted as if nudged by a ghostly hand. A slender crack divided them. An invitation.

Run! Mandrake's mind screamed. A door mysteriously opening never led to good things.

But something in him refused to let him go.

The Nose.

This was a mystery. He was hopeless to walk away.

Mandrake reached into his pocket and dialed 9-1-1. Curiosity didn't mean complete recklessness. He hovered his thumb over the 'Call' button. If someone did intend him harm, he could at least transmit a terrified scream to the authorities.

Mandrake threaded his body between the sliver of space between the doors, taking care to leave them open, assuming the inevitable quick getaway. The extra light spilling inside was a comforting bonus.

His feet shuffled along the filthy marble. If there was a foot chase he'd surely slip. The Seven really needed to invest in a maid.

The library appeared normal-ish. Its labyrinth of towering bookcases dimly lit by the flickering chandeliers gave off its usual Gothic ghost-story vibe, but anything other than the typical macabre feel would've triggered Mandrake's inner warning bells.

"Hello?" His voice echoed off the high ceiling.

Perhaps the door blew open from the breeze? It was wishful thinking, given the loud clack of its deadbolt.

It was possible the mystery door opener triggered the latch from the hidden headquarters beneath the building. Or maybe a snickering Abbey Prue hid in the shadows, readying to unleash an epic boo-scare.

The boy gritted his teeth. He hated being startled. His mind inventoried his recent beverage choices, instantly regretting the energy drink he had a mere hour ago. He steeled his bladder. "I know you're there. Locks don't unlock themselves."

The heavy doors crashed shut behind him. Mandrake leapt in fright. His phone squirted from his fingers and slid like a hockey puck across the grimy floor.

It was time to run for his life.

But a shadowy figure stood between him and his way out.

Tall, sharp, angled, he recognized the jaunty silhouette of Inspector Gunther Gates. A chill ran up his spine. Was it really Gates? Every goose bump on his body suggested otherwise.

"Mandrake Mandrake, I presume," Gates' deep voice boomed from the shadows. "You look like your father."

"You would know," Mandrake shot back before his better judgment stomped on the brakes.

The shadowy shape responded with chilly silence.

Mandrake rebooted the conversation. "What brings you here? The magazines? They've got a great selection. A little dated. But if you're looking for a 1974 Boy's Life, you've come to the right place."

The mysterious man strode out of the shadows. It was the Inspector all right, or at least an impossible to detect doppelganger. No hint of rubber or glue or makeup betrayed the authenticity of the crooked nose or the cadaver-white complexion, or the fan of wrinkles that spider-webbed from the edge of his eyes onto his veined temples. The disguise was so perfect. Doubts began to seep into Mandrake's thoughts.

Mandrake's gaze shifted to the Inspector's right eye and the round piece of glass squeezed between its cheek and brow.

The left eye, not the right. The correct eye. Had Max simply fixed his error since he'd walked out of Crime Island? Or could this be the actual Inspector?

"Is there something wrong?" The man took another step forward.

Mandrake retreated like some gym-class dance partner. The Inspector's unblinking gaze drooped to Mandrake's backpedaling feet, then rose again to meet the boy's wide-eyed stare.

"Uh, no. Just… a little warm for an overcoat, isn't it?" Mandrake dug his thumbs beneath the straps of his backpack. A hardback copy of The Inspector Speaks was still stuffed deep within. In someone else's possession the bag might be a deadly weapon of self-defense. In Mandrake's feeble C- for effort gym class hands, he might manage some spastic abomination of martial artistry, nothing more.

"There is no need for fear, young sir." The Inspector's crooked nose pointed at Mandrake like a witch's finger. "We are on the same side."

Mandrake's eyes searched for his fallen phone. A new strategy emerged — dive on the floor, grab the phone, hit send, scream to the 911 dispatcher.

Before he could move, the Inspector snatched the phone from the marble tile and raised it — "9-1-1" glowed in the glass of his monocled eye.

"I, uh, always keep that on speed dial. Just in case." He reached his hand out, inviting the Inspector to return his property.

The man tucked the phone into his overcoat's deep pocket. "Something's on your mind. Let's just get it out in the open. You've figured me out, have you?" The Inspector leaned forward until his nose practically pressed against Mandrake's.

Mandrake opened his mouth to talk but his tongue twisted into a useless tendril of pink meat.

The Inspector stared intensely. "You know my secret, don't you?"

Mandrake shook. "No. I don't know anything."

The Inspector clamped a heavy hand on Mandrake's shoulder. "Don't be shy, boy. I know your talents. I expected you'd see through my deception."

"My talents are rather untalented."

The Inspector plucked the monocle from his face and held it out between them. "What have you concluded from this cheap piece of glass?"

Mandrake pinched the lens and inspected it. "It's clear."

A half-smile stretched across the Inspector's taut cheeks. "Indeed."

"Your eye is fine. This does nothing."

The man circled Mandrake. "And now you're wondering why I wear it."

Mandrake had a good idea of why, but decided it safer not to tell. "Perhaps it's a fashion statement?"

The Inspector laughed a single, hardy laugh. "Yes. Of sorts. You've heard the tale of how I engaged in a duel with the Three Masked Swordteers? Of how my right cornea was scratched in the swordplay?"

Mandrake shrugged. "Maybe."

"It never happened. The Masked Swordteers were the most uncoordinated swashbucklers in the history of swashbuckling. They could barely see out of those ridiculous masks. They didn't scratch my eye. They're lucky they didn't poke their own eyes out with all that clumsy stabbing and swinging."

"But that story is in your book."

"Fiction," the Inspector snapped. "Even my appearance is mostly a costume. I enlisted the help of a Hollywood costume designer to create my signature look. He thought the monocle would add a touch of old-school traditionalism. Stupidest decision I ever made." He squeezed his fists. "I have to squeeze my cheek and eye brow to hold this worthless thing in place. With glasses your ears do all the work. But me? I get migraines. Sties. Temple cramping."

He massaged the sides of head with his fingertips. "And try chasing crooks without dropping it. Try getting punched in the face. Lawmen with glasses have it so easy."

Mandrake turned the monocle over in his hands. If the Inspector didn't need it to see, perhaps placing it in the wrong eye was a common mistake. Maybe it was just something he occasionally did to relieve his cramping cheek muscles. "Why are you here? And not on the helicopter with the rest?"

"I needed to talk to you." He leveled the boy with a chilly gaze. "Alone."

Blood drained from Mandrake's face. He blinked hard, trying to squeeze some juice back in his brain.

Amateur Sleuth Rule #26a

The Detective didn't do it.

Amateur Sleuth Rule #26b

If all of your suspects are detectives ignore rule 26a.

Amateur Sleuth Rule #26c

Don't kill anyone.
Otherwise we'll have to rethink rule 26a.

"The Sleuthing Seven has a traitor." Gates paced the library's mildewed carpet. "One of its members is in league with Max Mandrake."

A cauldron of uncertainty burned deep inside the boy detective. But he couldn't deny the idea wasn't plausible. The Seven kept him in the dark, after all. Maybe someone was scared he'd uncover their secret activities.

"You're good," the Inspector pointed at him. "But you have a lot to learn. The best detectives assume they never have all the answers. The greatest of us are open to other possibilities. We welcome them. We seek out help."

The words kicked Mandrake square in his over-inflated ego. Help? Mandrake had been trying so hard to be a solo act. Trying to get out of the shadow of Crash and the Chief and the Seven.

"Which is why I'm here. I need to get into the secret chamber. Someone has rearranged the books since I was last here. Probably our treacherous turncoat." His finger carved through a line of dusty bindings. "You can help."

"Oh... I... uh... don't know what you're talking about."

The Inspector whipped around. "Don't play coy with me, son. You wouldn't be here if they didn't show you their secret clubhouse. And you're far too smart to be outwitted by their silly tests."

"Yeah, well," Mandrake pondered his double-knotted shoelace. The skin of his cheeks felt like they were being warmed by a blow-dryer. "I wouldn't know about that."

"Ah. Maybe I misjudged. Maybe the others were right. They said you were all hype. They said you didn't have what it took."

"I have what it takes!" Mandrake balled his fists. "I solved their stupid puzzles. I even managed to sneak up on them. If anyone doesn't have what it takes, it's them."

Inspector Gates folded his arms and cocked a perfectly manicured brow.

Mandrake had been played. He needed to get it together. "I can't show you how to get in. It's a secret. I pinky swore."

"This is not some school yard game!" The Inspector grabbed him by the shoulders. "The city is in peril."

Mandrake tried to squirm away, but the Inspector's gloved hands immobilized him like handcuffs.

"Okay! I'll help!" Mandrake begged. "But first you have to do something for me."

The master detective glared at him, red-faced. He slid his sleeve back and checked his wrist watch. "What now? I don't have much time."

Mandrake's eyes narrowed. Why would a guy who named his silver timepiece wear a digital watch?

"What?!" the Inspector quickly covered it up.

"Nothing." Mandrake whipped his backpack off. He pulled out the hardback copy of The Inspector Speaks and a pen."Was just hoping I could get an autograph."

The Inspector gave a judgmental chuckle and snatched the book away. He began to open it.

"On the cover!" Mandrake shouted. "On the cover. Right on your stunningly handsome picture. Make it out to Manny. That's my nickname."

Gates gritted his teeth, snatched the pen and slashed his signature in a quick flourish, then slammed the book shut and poked it at Mandrake. "There you go, Manny. I better not find that on the Internet."

"No sir." Mandrake studied the signature:

To Manny, with love and hugs, Inspector Gunther Gates.

The capital letters were tall and ornate, almost Calligraphy, something an artist would do.

"Is something wrong?" the Inspector asked.

"I just don't want to smear the ink." Mandrake blew on it and strategically turned his back to the Inspector. He snuck a peek at the first page, secretly comparing the actual signature of Inspector Gunther Gates to the fresh one.

They were different. For one, the new signature used the full name including Gunther while the original one only used two large looping letters — "GG" abbreviating Gunther Gates.

The G's of the original were scribbles, almost hieroglyphics, nothing like the carefully plotted lettering of this new autograph.

Mandrake's breath quickened. He was now convinced that for the first time in his young life, he was standing in the presence of his villainous father.

"Now," the Inspector said. "Open the secret door."

The Inspector paid close attention as Mandrake's shaky hands wrestled the book into his bag.

"Yes, of course," Mandrake's voice quavered. "Stand right here. The trap door is here."

The Inspector stared at his feet. "Here?"

"Yes," Mandrake nodded. "The book that triggers it is on the other side of the bookcase. That's the puzzle. You have to pull a book from one side, but get back here in time."

"Impossible!"

"Impossible is a word that should be in no Detective's vocabulary."

The Inspector squinted. Mandrake was certain he was on to him.

"Just wait here." Mandrake scuttled off, making a tight U-Turn around the corner of the shelf. Alone, Mandrake closed his eyes and leaned against the shelf.

"What's going on back there?" His father's disguised voice called through the bookcase.

Mandrake flattened his hands on the thick books of the shelf. "Just about to give you what you deserve. Be sure you're close to the book case."

Mandrake pushed. His muscles flexed. His chest tightened. An instinctual grunt barked from his chest. "Here it comes!"

But the shelf didn't budge.

Not an inch.

It didn't even creak.

"Everything okay over there?" the faux Inspector queried.

"Yeah," Mandrake said between deep gulps of air. "Book's a bit stuck. Just stay where you are. Don't move."

Mandrake squatted and dug his shoulder into the shelf. He pushed hard with his legs, putting every ounce of middle school muscle he had into it.

Nothing.

Nada.

The shelf didn't even jiggle.

"Need some help?" the Inspector suddenly loomed behind him.

"Uh..." Mandrake dashed for the door but a strong hand grabbed the back of his collar and ripped him backward.

The Inspector — aka Max Mandrake — raised him up like one would lift a small rabbit by the scruff of the neck. A demented, very un-Inspector like smile adorned the villain's face. "So... You know who I am?"

The boy detective spied the Inspector's pocket. It betrayed the square indentation of Mandrake's phone.

The villain scooped it out. "You want this? For what? To call for help? No one can help you, child. Not now." Max stuck his face right into Mandrake's. "How did you figure me out? The security video?"

"Yeah. It was this." Mandrake flicked his finger into the monocle. PANG!

Max flinched and dropped Mandrake.

Mandrake snatched his phone from the trench coat pocket and raced to the front door. A plan formulating in his mind. Get outside! Scream for help! Dial 911!

He grabbed the brass door handles and tugged. They didn't budge. He's was locked in!

Behind him, boots slapped the floor.

Mandrake ducked into the new fiction section.

A voice bled through the bookcases. "Enough of this kid. Come out here, so we can finally meet."

Mandrake held his breath. He guessed his father was in the next row over. His shaky fingers dialed 9-1-1. He pressed the phone to his ear.

"I can hear you dialing," the voice hissed through the books. "It's too late for that. The police have their hands full about now."

The phone rang and rang. 9-1-1 wasn't answering. Something was seriously wrong.

"You are a bright boy." Max was closer now. "You remind me of me."

"I'm nothing like you." Mandrake blurted then slapped his hand over his mouth. Stupid move! Max was just trying to lure him out and Mandrake had fallen right into his trap.

Mandrake ducked deeper into the labyrinth of titles. He could hear Max stalking him from the other side. "If you knew it was me all this time, why didn't you run to the 'good guys'?"

Mandrake imagined the sinister smile on the villain's lips.

"I get it, kid." Max chuckled. "Why should they take all the credit for your hard work, eh?"

Mandrake felt moistness in his eyes. What had he done?! All this time, he was lying to himself, saying what he did was for the good of the city. But he was as selfish as anyone. He removed his glasses and dried his teary eyes.

When he put them back on, there stood Max Mandrake. The mask of the Inspector was gone. "Or maybe, you didn't want to give up your dad. We're blood after all. Blood doesn't betray blood."

"No! You're wrong. I hate you. And everything you're about." He turned to run but Max grabbed his arm.

"I'm not what you think. I can prove it. In the headquarters, there's a red envelope. I need what's inside it."

"I don't believe anything you say."

"It's behind the shark aquarium. There's an old treasure chest."

"I'd never help you."

"I'm afraid you have no choice." The villain moved to scoop him up.

Suddenly, the bookcase to Max's right tipped. It crashed down on the Man, burying him under hundreds of hardbacks.

And there on the other side of the bookcase stood —

"Grandma?"

Amateur Sleuth Rule #27

Fake it till you make it...

Grandma raised her varicose veined leg and karate kicked the library's double-doors open. Wood splintered. Sun blasted in.

Despite the sudden assault of light, Mandrake's eyelids refused to blink. His jaw slackened but his sudden state of shock made speech impossible. Was this a hallucination? A lucid dream? Some elaborate Max Mandrake con job?

On most nights, Grandma wobbled around the house with a therapeutic cane. She barely had the mobility to wrestle her doctor prescribed circulatory stockings over her ankles. Her go-to jewelry was the "Home Alert" bracelet which could summon an ambulance in any "I've fallen and I can't get up" situation.

She just ninja kick her way through eight-inches of dead-bolted hickory.

This was no ordinary Grandma!

Grandma whisked Mandrake down the concrete steps. Her car was parked at the decaying curb. Mandrake slid inside, his butt squeaking across the pleather seat, as the heavy door crunched shut. Grandma slid across the hood like some TV cop in a muumuu.

"How is this happening?" Mandrake said.

Grandma stuck the landing, did a little spin and sardined herself behind the steering wheel.

"Seat belts," she grunted then slammed her door shut.

The tires squealed. The smell of burning rubber bled into Mandrake's nose. The car blasted ahead, leaving the Baker Street Library in its gravely dust.

"Grandma!" Mandrake scrambled to strap in. "What's happening?"

Grandma's cataract gray eyes peered ahead. "We need to get out of the city. There's danger here."

"Danger?" Mandrake waved back to the library. "You just buried the danger in a pile of almanacs."

Grandma shifted gears and roared through traffic. "Don't underestimate Max Mandrake. He's a vile schemer. "

Mandrake braced his arms against the dashboard. He'd never even seen her drive the speed limit, let alone 40-mph above it. "Grandma, what you did back there. The way you slid across the car. The way you're driving. That's not the work of an Octogenarian."

"Adrenaline." Grandma elbow dropped the door lock.

"You're too old for adrenaline. You can't even stay awake past six-thirty." Mandrake said. "Tell me the truth. I'm a kid sleuth you know. I can tell when people are lying. I can smell it... "

Grandma squeezed her armpits close to her body, trapping any liar flop sweat. She slipped off her glasses and rested them on the dashboard. "It's time I stopped molly-coddling you."

"Is that another word for 'lying to'?" Mandrake said.

"Protecting." Grandma lifted a folder labeled "The Argyll School of Art" and placed it on the dash. "I called the school at Poodle Springs. You're going there tomorrow. I made a special arrangement."

"I can't go there. Not now."

"Enough! It's not a discussion —"

"You're not my mother!"

Grandma sunk back into the driver's seat. The worn upholstery almost hugging her. Mandrake had crossed a line. A hiss of air escaped from her nose, as if she needed to decompress lest she explode. "Mindy — your mother — isn't what those books say. She was more than some mustache-twirling villain."

"She had a mustache?! No wonder she went evil."

"No doofus! She didn't have a mustache! It's just a thing people say! And she wasn't evil either." Grandma stared off. "She just got sick of being taken advantage of. She tried to be a movie star. She studied hard. Hustled. Gave it everything she had. She just wanted to see her name in lights."

"How did she become... corrupt?"

"She took a shortcut. The longest distance between two points is always a shortcut. Things snowballed." Grandma took her eyes off the road to lock him in an icy stare. "The truth is, I'm y—"

"GRANDMA!" Mandrake screamed. They were speeding toward a wall of stopped cars.

SKREEEECH!!! Grandma stomped on the brakes. Her right forearm whacked Mandrake's chest like a safety-bar made of meat.

They skidded to a stop mere millimeters from a semi-truck's rear bumper.

Horns squealed. Fists shook. A parade of gridlocked vehicles stretched out in front of them. Grandma slapped her glasses back on. They were trapped in this maze of metal.

"Run for your lives!!! They're coming!!" a wild-eyed man shouted as he jumped from car hood to car hood. "No one is safe!"

A family, two cars ahead, abandoned their minivan, snatched some hastily-packed luggage from their backseat, and scampered up the street on foot, racing past an alley where a stuffy businessman in an expensive suit dove inside a dumpster and closed the lid.

A cop pushed a kid off a tricycle and pedaled away.

"What's going on?" Mandrake stared up at the sky, spying for earth-killing asteroids.

"There's been an escape at Crime Island!" a frazzled woman cried as she sprinted in front of the car. The five cats gathered in her arms clawed at her face.

"Oh, that." Mandrake straightened. "Old news. I figured out Max

Mandrake escaped a few days ago."

Grandma shot him with a sideways glance. "Nobody's ever more surprised than a know-it-all."

"I'm not a know-it-all," Mandrake snapped. "I'm a know-a-lot."

"Then you should know it's not just Max Mandrake that's flown the coop." Grandma squeezed the wheel tight and glared ahead as if waiting for some break in the clogged road to open. "All of the prisoners of that godforsaken place escaped."

"That's not possible." Mandrake's face felt hot. His eyes shifted to the car's vents, wondering if Grandma had cranked the heat on.

"The news just broke. It said that Inspector Gates led a team of detectives to the prison on some kind of mission. They were tricked. The prisoners stole their helicopter."

The helicopter. Mandrake's pulse quickened. "But what about the prison guards in the towers?"

"The morning shift guards were abducted at their homes and replaced with imposters."

Mandrake remembered the portraits of the guards that decorated Max's drab cell. His father had been studying their features to find the perfect doppelgangers.

"The inmates stole the helicopter," Grandma continued. "Now, they're loose in the city."

Mandrake stared out at the chaos raging around him. He had caused this. If he had confessed all he knew to the Seven from the start this wouldn't be happening. If he would've worked as a team player, there would be no mass hysteria in the streets.

"Where are the detectives now?" he asked.

"They haven't been seen since they stepped inside the prison."

Mandrake's stomach was suddenly queasy. "But if they're gone, who can stop the escaped criminals?"

Grandma's lips quivered. "No one."

Mandrake sunk in his seat, as if the guilt within him added five pounds to his frail frame. "I have to go back. I know what he wants. There's an envelope inside a treasure chest. If I get it —"

"You'll be playing right into his hands," Grandma grunted. "You think playing detective with Crash Brickfist has prepared you to do battle with the greatest villain of all time?"

Her openness shocked him. She never talked about her daughter or Max. "You knew about my sleuthing all this time? Crash? The library?"

"You're a terrible liar. Which just makes it all worse." Grandma shook her head. "Good guys don't lie."

"They do if they're lying for good."

"You think Max Mandrake started out kidnapping the President's Chihuahua? Or stealing the hubcaps off the Pope Mobile? Or filling the Grand Canyon with Jell-O?"

"Jell-O? He did that? I never —"

"That's not the point." Grandma slammed her hands against the dash.

"I heard he was a crime-fighter once. What changed him?"

"Being a know-it-all." Grandma frowned. "But it's not too late for you. You may have some of his brilliance, but you don't have to make his mistakes. It doesn't matter who your parents are. They're not you. You make the path. You choose."

The words summoned goosebumps on Mandrake's skin. He took in the chaos around him. Had he caused this? His lies? His selfishness?

"Max started small, with little secrets and tiny deceptions. Villains always think they're the heroes."

"I'm not the only one who keeps secrets, am I?"

"I'm your Grandmother."

"Then tell me – when you and Crash Brickfist had that private conversation, what did he tell you? Why did you let me go?"

Grandma pressed her lips together, at a loss for words. She wanted to tell him something, but she couldn't.

"That's what I thought," Mandrake turned away. His eyes wandered to a TV store. Inside, every TV in the store shouted out a bold text graphic. "SPECIAL MESSAGE FROM MAX MANDRAKE!!"

Grandma turned the knob of the car radio.

The audio was synced to the televisions. Music played, the kind of music that heralded snowstorms, declarations of war and celebrity divorces.

The screens cut to the local newsroom where Max Mandrake sat smugly behind the anchor's desk, drumming his fingers.

"Guess who's back..." Max grinned. "I'm sure you've missed me. Well, fear not my cowering public, I've been planning a big caper for your enjoyment. One for the books. To make up for lost time."

Images of the city in chaos flashed on the screen.

Max's voice played over them, "I've unleashed the world's greatest crooks and bad boys on your precious city. Somebody had to liven things up! You know their names and you know the devastation they'll cause." Max paused for dramatic effect. "But there's more!"

The screen showed a series of images of the Sleuthing 7, locked in cells at Crime Island. "I've captured the greatest detectives of our time and locked them in Crime Island. So, who will save Capital City?"

Mandrake closed his eyes and dug his fingers into the seat upholstery. This was the worst-case scenario.

"Here's the deal. I'll unleash my sleuthing crime fighter prisoners for one billion dollars. Cash money! The money is to be delivered to the old East Side docks by midnight."

Max cackled. "If I don't have that money by midnight tonight, you'll never see them again."

The television cut to a shot of Crime Island, apparently filmed from one of the tall sniper towers.

"The decision is yours. How much are your detectives worth, Capital City?" The images of the city in chaos returned. "Don't be cheap."

The television signal cut and an announcer voice came on — "NOW BACK TO OUR UNSCHEDULED ENDLESS MARATHON OF ARNOLD THE TERRIBLE."

Mandrake closed his eyes. He was responsible. He needed to clean it up. He had to get that envelope.

Mandrake clutched the door handle, shoved the door open, and went to dive out of the car. "Gaaaaarg!" If only he hadn't forgotten to unbuckle his seatbelt. The upper half of it strangled him, as the bottom half bit into his belly.

"What stupid thing are you doing now?" Grandma tilted her head.

"Um...saving the city." He clicked the seatbelt's release button, but Grandma snatched his wrist with a strength he never imagined she possessed until about an hour ago.

"This city isn't worth it, boy." Tears were in Grandma's eyes. "Take it from someone who knows."

"After I'm done, we'll talk," Mandrake said. "I'm sorry."

"Sorry? For what?"

Mandrake raised his leg and stomped down on the gas pedal. The car lurched into the truck in front of them. Steel met steel. Grandma whipped back to the wheel, pure instinct, releasing Mandrake from her grasp. The boy flung himself sidewise out of the car. His flailing arms softened the impact. He didn't have time for pain. He rolled away and ran off down the street.

He didn't look back, he didn't have to. She'd be after him. He had seen enough to realize those arthritic knees had enough burst to catch him if he hesitated for even a second.

He dove inside the flatbed of a pickup truck and covered himself with what looked like an old horse blanket. His chest heaved. He sucked in some deep breaths, trying to calm his racing lungs. He'd give it a few minutes to make sure the coast was clear then he'd return to the Baker Street Library to find the thing so important to Max Mandrake that he escaped from an inescapable prison just to get it.

AMATEUR SLEUTH RULE #28

Don't shoot your eye out.

THE HAND-WRITTEN SIGN TAPED to the archaic treasure chest displayed an ominous message: "EXTREME DANGER — DO NOT OPEN!"

Mandrake sighed. More extreme danger? Really? What a day!

Returning to the Baker Street Library was risky. He wagered that Max no longer lurked among the rows of books, too busy hijacking the local television station and threatening to kill the Sleuthing Seven.

He put his intuition to the test by sneaking through the shadows and triggering the trap door in the criminology section without being ambushed.

But reaching the underground Headquarters did little to calm Mandrake's jitters. Max busted out of an inescapable prison to obtain something in this secret lair. He'd be back. Soon.

Mandrake had found the old pirate treasure chest exactly where Max had told him — hidden behind the shark aquariums.

The fact that this seemingly harmless trunk warranted a danger sign, but the tank filled with vicious man-eating fish did not, gave Mandrake serious pause. Dead Mandrake couldn't save the city.

He needed protection. He decided to strap on the ancient suit of armor. He doubted the ironclad suit that stood sentry outside the main conference room was actually meant to be worn. Even lifting a single metal boot required a physical strength people shelled out good money for at the local YMCA.

Even worse, the armor was meant for an adult-sized knight. He did his best to piece together steel chunks, using them to cover his important bits.

He donned the helmet last. His panting breath hissed against its suffocating iron. It smelled pungent and left a metallic taste in his mouth, like he'd been sucking on pennies. Hopefully, it wasn't dangerous. He doubted they knew about things like lead poisoning in medieval times.

Mandrake estimated the armor would protect him against an explosion or a venom tipped dart. It wouldn't do much good if a giant dragon leapt out or the ghosts of Blackbeard "arrrghed" from its depths.

Mandrake reached out with the armored glove, wedged his steel thumbs under the latch, and flipped it up.

His relieved breath filled the claustrophobic space of the helmet. All his limbs were still in place and he didn't smell any poisonous gas.

He closed his eyes and opened the lid.

Creeeeeak.

He was still alive. That was a plus.

He leaned over and gazed inside.

The treasure chest was empty. Completely. Not even a bottom.

In fact, it wasn't a chest at all. It was a hatch that opened to a deep dark pit.

His eyes adjusted to the black nothingness. He needed a flashlight, but his phone rested snugly behind the metal codpiece that adorned his nether regions. Retrieving it would require a bucket of oil and a can opener.

No time for that. Mandrake climbed inside the rotten wood frame. He hung from the top. His rusty boots dangled into the empty blackness.

He closed his eyes and let go.

CLANK! His steel feet hit metal. He stood on the roof of a rusted out subway car. His eyes adjusted. He gazed ahead. A seemingly endless stretch of abandoned Capital Metro tunnel greeted him. A few feet ahead, an open lead to the interior of the car. He climbed inside, his toes again hitting solid ground. He looked down to see what he was standing on.

Books.

Tall stacks of them, some reaching all the way to the train car's ceiling. Mandrake scrambled between them. There were thousands of paperbacks crammed into the tight space, all of them identical. He grabbed one and wiped the dust from its cover. The face of Inspector Gunther Gates stared back. He read the familiar bold lettered title — The Inspector Speaks. Second Edition!

He laughed to himself. This book seemed to be following him.

While he was tempted to read, the secrets buried within the Inspector's memoir didn't compare to finding the mysterious red envelope and knowing why Max Mandrake needed to possess it.

He tucked the copy into his backpack for later and wedged his way through the towers of paperbacks, toward the front of the car.

A glimmer of light caught his attention. An animated screen saver projecting from a clunky old computer lit an aged and clutter-filled desk.

It was an older computer – at least five years old – clunky and large with a mouse and no scratchpad. He clicked the spacebar, revealing the computer's desktop. Mandrake quickly surveyed its displayed app icons — a word processor, a calculator, a web-browser.

But the last one caught his eye – MAX-A-MORPH. Mandrake gasped. Max-A-Morph was the name of the super-secret disguise technology Max used to commit a host of his most sinister crimes. What was the Inspector doing with it? Officially, no one knew how Max's technology worked, even now.

But unofficially...

Max double-clicked the icon, summoning a computer window with a list of "MORPHS":

Guard12v3

Guard2v6

Inspectorv7

OldLadyM6463

Mandrake clicked the Inspector one — a 3D schematic of the Inspector popped up on the screen. The details were astonishing. Only the weird wrist-watch — instead of the Inspector's classic timepiece — seemed out of place.

Beneath the list a red button labeled "Begin Render" appeared.

Mandrake hit the button.

VOOOOOOOOOOOM! A refrigerator-sized black box hummed like an airplane engine. Red light emanated from deep inside it. Lasers, Mandrake guessed. The box shook and groaned. A twisty nest of snakelike cables and wires sparked.

Mandrake turned back to the computer. A message box covered most of the screen — "RENDER TIME 26 Hours and 40 minutes."

Mandrake tried to shut down the process, but he couldn't click around the new information window. He debated shutting the computer down but worried he might break something important to the Inspector.

He sighed and turned his attention elsewhere on the desk. He picked through unpaid bills, autographed photographs of the Inspector, envelopes and correspondence.

Mandrake lifted a handwritten letter on top of the pile. The stationary's header was printed — CAPITAL HOUSE PUBLISHING.

He read on:

Dear Inspector,

Book sales are dismal. We're cancelling future printings. Readers are bored of crime and villains. However, they do love cats. If you have a story about crime-fighting cats, we'll do lunch.

Sincerely,
J.K. Fowler, Editor, Capital House Publishing

Mandrake crumbled the paper and tossed it in the wastebasket. It bounced off something red. Something envelope-ey.

The red envelope!

Mandrake's heartbeat pounded out a heavy metal drum-solo in his ears. He twisted off the tin helmet, allowing the cool subterranean air to greet his sweat-glistened face. Booby-trap or not, he needed to see this with his own medieval visor-less eyes.

He grabbed it. Across the front, written in thick black ink, were the words "MANUSCRIPT — FINAL DRAFT".

Mandrake flipped it over, focusing on the envelope's bendable clasp. It was undone. Opened. Empty!

"No!" He shuddered. Someone had beaten him here.

Mandrake crumbled the envelope in anger. He had nothing.

He paced, his knight footwear clanging off the floor.

Sure, he could track down whoever had beaten him here, but he had precious few hours to rescue the Sleuthing Seven. There was still one other thing Max wanted — the ransom! One billion dollars!

Mandrake fought off tears, worried about rusting up his current outfit. He was a detective, not a banker. Getting a billion dollars wasn't his forte.

If only he were... a villain!

He clapped his hands. What would Max Mandrake do?

The thought revolted him. But Abbey might be right. Perhaps his special talent wasn't just an ability to anticipate the schemes of criminal geniuses but instead an innate knack for formulating his own diabolical master-plans.

Where could he get a lot of money fast?

He had some ideas. But first, he needed help.

AMATEUR SLEUTH RULE #29

In the real world, you won't fit in the air vent... try the door.

A LONE MOP STOOD INSIDE a sudsy bucket in the desolate middle-school hallway. A fresh circle of soapy dampness surrounded it. Its mop jockey had left in a hurry.

"Hello?" Mandrake's call echoed off the lockers.

No reply came.

This was eerie. Janitors never abandoned their posts. They rode out blizzards and floods, scrubbed urinals on unairconditioned summer days, and even hunkered down and bleached desks and chairs on Christmas and New Year's and 4th of July.

Things were truly dire.

An hour had passed since Mandrake put out the call. He didn't have a fully formulated plan yet, but he knew with the right people he'd figure this out.

If they showed up.

Showing up was no small matter. On his long walk back to the school, Mandrake witnessed a city under siege. He was surprised it hadn't spilled over to the school, and assumed it was only a matter of time. Mandrake squeezed inside his locker and eased the door shut.

He pulled out his phone and opened his 'TODO' app. His fingers typed.

SAVE THE CITY TODO LIST:

Step 1: Get a Billion Dollars...

His eyes drooped. What was step 2? Or for that matter, how was he going to get a billion dollars?

He erased step 1 and replaced it with:

Step 1: Gather a team... who knows how to get a billion dollars.

Step 2: Save the City.

Step 3:

Zzzzzzzzzzzzzzz.

He fell asleep. In his defense, it had been a long couple of days of breaking curfews, solving crimes and escaping near-death situations. He'd earned a nap.

THUNK! His head hit the inside of the locker. He rubbed his noggin, hoping it wouldn't welt up. He needed to be on his game for when the team arrived. Huge noggin lumps didn't inspire confidence. Neither did snoring.

He needed to stay awake.

Mandrake unzipped his backpack and picked through its contents. He'd tucked away one of the thousand copies of The Inspector Speaks he swiped from the abandoned subway car beneath the library. The Inspector wasn't going to miss it.

He skipped to Chapter 13, the very section his grandmother diligently redacted with her thick black marker in his previous copy.

Laying his eyes on the unfiltered text felt like a deep betrayal. But this was bigger than him or Grandma. This was about saving the city!

He read on...

AMATEUR SLEUTH RULE #30

When talking about cases always use alliteration. For example - *The Case of the Egyptian's Parents* is inherently less interesting than *The Case of the Mummy's Mommy.*

EXCERPT FROM THE INSPECTOR SPEAKS:

CHAPTER 13

The question I, Inspector Gunther Gates, am most often asked is: "How do you get your magnificent chin so square and chiseled?"

But the second most often-asked question is — "what did it take to bring down Capitol City's most brilliant criminal mastermind?"

The answer is simple. An even more brilliant criminal mastermind... with a perfectly chiseled square chin.

Brilliance is a curse I've suffered since an early age. I read my first book at four months — Agatha Christie's Murder on the Orient Express. I published my first book of sonnets at age three. I cured an incurable disease for my third grade science fair project.

(Diareheaeluenzaitous. Never heard of it? You're welcome.)

Sure, I would've preferred to do normal kid stuff like working at a law firm or winning Olympic medals.

But the world expected more of me.

Max Mandrake had a similar childhood. He grew up with a need to keep topping himself. This ambition extended to his villainy. His incredible need to do the impossible led him down the wrong path.

He needed a challenge.

He wouldn't find it in ordinary law enforcement.

I was in a similar predicament. My biggest weakness had always been my fabulousness.

It's hard to find a worthy test when you're near perfect.

At the time, I was in a funk. To put it in perspective, three days had passed since I sent my trademark London Fog overcoat to the dry cleaners. My custom Italian shoes had not been shined in three days.

I can only imagine how the infamous Max Mandrake's own wardrobe had suffered the devastating effects of unchecked wonderfulness.

Whether it was the pressure to commit the crime of the century or just a need to right his own sense of fashion, Max Mandrake was about to make the biggest mistake of his life.

Capital City was the toast of the world that week, as host of the Incredible Bowl, professional football's largest event. Every year, the league voted on a city to hold the big game. Every other year, Capital City was the choice. It made sense. Capital City was the center of the world for commerce, entertainment, media, sports… .

… and crime.

The Incredible Bowl was like a holiday. The world stopped. Crime rates dropped 99% during the actual event. Crooks were too busy eating chicken wings and chili to rob and pillage.

Only a brilliant criminologist like myself could wade through the veil of sports ecstasy, and see the event for what it truly was — criminal catnip.

A prudent crook would use the game as a distraction, striking somewhere else while everyone's attention was focused on the national spectacle.

But Max Mandrake wasn't some mere bank jobber. He was an artist of the illegal. He yearned for a stage and there was none bigger than Capital City's Starfish Tuna Stadium (aka the Tuna Can).

I planned accordingly, laid my trap, and waited.

I also plunked down a huge bet on the Baltimore Blitz. Their stingy defense and clock-eating run game seemed like the right recipe for a world championship.

The pregame ceremonies went as planned. A pop singer over-sang the anthem. Expensive commercials with dogs and fancy cars and the latest summer blockbusters invaded people's homes.

The game — billed as a battle of equals — quickly became a laugher. The stingy Baltimore Blitz defense gave up touchdowns. Their usual sure-handed quarterback was fumbling the ball.

By half time, the heavily favored Baltimore Blitz was down 44-7, their lone touchdown coming on a klutzy interception thrown by the Texas Thunder's rookie quarterback.

The Blitz weren't playing like themselves.

And that's when I realized, they weren't themselves.

Or at least, MVP Quarterback Johnny Colt wasn't.

During half time, I used one of my Vegas connections to confirm that before the game started, someone had laid a multi-million dollar bet against the Baltimore Blitz.

With the enormous odds in favor of Baltimore, the mysterious better stood to make a killing.

Which is why I aimed my binoculars at Johnny Colt. He looked like the quarterback I'd seen on TV shows and highlight films. But I was convinced he was an impostor.

Max Mandrake had kidnapped Johnny Colt and replaced him. The villain was playing quarterback for the Baltimore Blitz!

Many have questioned why, if I knew Max Mandrake was making a mockery of the most watched sporting extravaganza of the year, I didn't apprehend him before the third-quarter kicked off. Some have suggested my monetary stake in the game influenced my call to action that night.

To them I say, "Poppycock!"

As evidence of my virtue, I offer Max Mandrake's crimes. First, Mandrake's level of mimicry was far beyond spirit gum and fake mustachery. His disguise was accurate down to the fingerprint level. His so-called Max-a-Morph technology was so precise it required an intense medical examination just to unmask him. Consider the time it would take to get a sitting judge on a night when EVERYONE was watching the event of the year to authorize the apprehension and clinical examination of the world's most popular and recognized athlete on the very night of his biggest failure and you'll see what I was up against.

In further defense, I'd propose that the capture of a criminal mastermind as dastardly as Max Mandrake far outweighs any sporting event... even the most popular one of the year.

I quickly came up with a plan. I knew Mandrake would attempt to collect his winnings immediately after the game. There was only one gambling establishment willing to take bets as large as Max Mandrake's – the Castle Casino.

I staked out the Casino for hours. My fingers developed blisters from pulling the handles on the slot machines.

Finally, someone arrived to pick up the money.

The bag man wasn't Max Mandrake. In fact, it was no man at all.

It was his wife and partner in crime, Mindy Mandrake. Mindy wasn't the brains behind the operation, she was the muscle. Even as able at fisticuffs as I was, I knew I couldn't defeat Mindy Mandrake in hand-to-hand combat. Mindy had trained as a Hollywood stunt-woman before Max Mandrake swept her into a life of crime. She was an expert of numerous martial arts and held Guinness records for jumping off buildings and surviving explosions.

She wasn't someone you approached without a cunning plan.

Lucky for me, I was a master of such plans.

Due to the traffic of the post-game activities — I knew there was only one route out of Capital City that night.

The Briar Street Bridge.

The Briar Street Bridge was the newest public works project set in motion by the Capital City development committee. Intended to be a six-lane super bridge, construction had started ten years prior to that night, but funding had fallen short, and the platform was incomplete, still a near 30 feet short of the shore.

Most people would consider the Briar Street Bridge a dead end, but for a renowned Hollywood stunt-woman turned criminal, Mindy Mandrake would have considered it a chance to break her personal record of distance jumping in a car.

Mindy, like her husband, was a serial showoff.

I parked my car, positioning it sideways, ninety degrees, stretching across the center of the bridge. I placed myself firmly at the middle of the roadblock. My trusty Luger pistol in hand.

And I waited.

Within minutes, the black supercharger roared down the road, Mindy at the wheel, Max Mandrake counting his winnings. I can only imagine their sheer terror as they spotted me, their arch nemesis, two steps ahead of them on the bridge.

Less courageous men would claim their lives flash before them in such a predicament. Not me. My pulse rate didn't budge. My thoughts drifted only slightly to what the future might be if I failed to bring down these master-villains right then.

I drew my weapon and fired two shots into the smoking tires.

The rubber exploded. The brakes screamed. Mindy steered the car into a controlled swerve.

But not controlled enough.

Her bumper slammed into the rails. Glass shattered. Her seatbelt must have been unlatched – defiant to the end – the concussion of hitting the bridge headfirst hurled her through the windshield and plunged her off the bridge, to certain death.

Despite the horrifying sight, I kept calm. There was still one more supervillain to deal with. I approached the smashed and smoking car with caution.

Max Mandrake leapt out, trying to take me by surprise, knives in each hand. But he was the one that would be surprised. I unleashed a pair of surgically placed judo chops, disarming him, then fired a third fist to his head, knocking him unconscious.

And with that, the reign of the most dastardly villain in Capital City history was over.

I clicked a pair of cuffs around his wrists in triumph, as a soft noise tickled my ears.

In the utter silence of the bridge that night, I followed the sound back to the car.

It was crying. A baby.

Inside, latched inside a child's car seat was the young baby, no more than six months old –

Mandrake Mandrake.

"HELP ME!!!" A cry interrupted Mandrake's reading. He pushed his legs, sliding up against the cramped locker wall.

The scream came again — "SOMEONE PLEASE HELP!"

Amateur Sleuth Rule #31

Never say "Perhaps you're wondering why I've called you all here... "

"AAAAAAH!! Someone save me!" The cries of horror echoed down the hall.

Mandrake followed the screams, fearing the worst. The escaped villains must have converged on the middle-school. He wasn't sure what he'd do against a fully-adult, fully-evil gang of escaped convicts. But ignoring a scream of someone in need was against his personal code. Not that he ever wrote one down or anything. That would be crazy-town.

Mandrake tried dialing the police again, but all circuits were busy.

As he huffed and puffed his way to the scene, Mandrake decided his best bet was to take the villains by surprise, to run into whatever ugly situation he was about to encounter and improvise.

He let out a battle cry, raced around the corner and was blocked by six feet of solid flab.

The Ox. His face burned red with anger. His bully-raged eyes bulged and wild-boar nostrils flared.

Luckily, the brute was occupied. The shrieks of terror that called Mandrake here emanated from the mouth of poor Billy Doocy, who was being dunked in a trashcan like a donut in coffee.

"You think it's funny, Dookie?" Ox asked. "Dookie" was the name Ox hung on Billy a year ago. It was likely the last thing Billy typically heard before his underwear was stretched over his ears. "You think you can trick me?!"

"Please Mr. Ox! I didn't call you here! I thought you were expelled.

I would never bother you on your day off."

Ox raised Billy by the ankles, til they were face to face. "Got a call. Told me to come here and find out who framed me. And here you are."

Recalling the dirty trick with the prison surveillance video Dookie, uh, Doocy pulled on him, Mandrake considered letting this middle-grade torture session carry out a bit longer, but his good-guy instincts kicked in. Stupid code.

"Ox!" Mandrake stepped out, putting himself in Ox's line of fire. "Step away from that audio-visual club member."

Ox smiled sinisterly. "This is getting better. Like Bully Christmas."

"Billy didn't set you up." Mandrake said. "It was me."

"Grrrrrrrrrrrrrrrrrrrrr," Ox grrred.

"Uh, I appreciate the clearing of the air," Billy said, from his upside down position. "We shouldn't make the violent Swirlie-proned middle schooler angry until after he safely puts me down on dry land."

"Ox, I'm here to help." Mandrake held up his hands defensively. "I can get you back in school."

Ox stepped toward Mandrake, swinging Billy forward. "Too late Mandrake. Lestrade already called me. He's bringing me back. He said —"

"— it's not the same school without you?" Mandrake dropped his voice an octave while sucking in his gut, and scrunching his face like the vice principal. "Meet me at the school in ten minutes. We need to figure this out. I'll even throw in free strawberry milk for lunch."

Billy cocked his ear. "Waitaminute! I recognize that voice! It sounds like the cop who invited me here to —"

"—pick up your key to the city." Mandrake affected the voice again.

"Wow," Billy said. "Are you a psychic? Did you tap my phone? Did you tap the psychic's phone?"

Ox shook Billy. "It's him, you idiot. Mandrake tricked us."

"Whoa now.'Trick' is such a loaded word. This is more like an invitation. Like to a surprise party." Mandrake waved his hands festively. "Surprise."

"You should put me down." Billy clutched his stomach. "Harder to pummel Mandrake if you have to hold me over your head the whole time."

Ox stuffed Billy headfirst into the trashcan, rolled up his sleeves and turned to Mandrake. "You're gonna pay."

"I'm telling the truth. I can get you back into the school!"

"Why do you think I'd want back into this stupid place?"

Mandrake bumped into the lockers. There was nowhere left to retreat. "There's a reason why you never passed seventh grade. You know the material better than anyone. All those years in school. All those days in detention. You can pass seventh grade. You could probably teach it. You're scared of high-school."

"I'm not scared of anything," Ox growled.

"Oh? What about all those kids you bullied when they were little eleven-year-old weaklings? The ones who are now in the twelfth grade and had crazy growth spurts and play football? They'd all love to get revenge on you, wouldn't they? There, you wouldn't be a big dog. You'd be a chew-toy."

Ox's lips quivered. "You don't know what you're talking about."

"I can fix it," Mandrake said. "You can finally go to high school. And not be bullied. Not be scared."

Ox's eyes narrowed to thin slits. Mandrake had his attention.

"Hm. I might be interested." Ox cracked his knuckles. "But first, I'm going to stick you in the dumpster. On principle. Bully ethics."

Mandrake braced for the attack.

"Guard the groin, Mandrake!" Billy dragged himself up from the trashcan to watch the spectacle. "Don't be a hero!"

Ox grabbed Mandrake's shirt and drew him close. "Prepare to be Ox-ed!"

A lightning bolt of plaid shot across the hall. A knee-high sock slammed into the front of Ox's ankles, sweeping his feet and flipping him over. Ox's face high-fived the floor.

His attacker, Abbey Prue, loomed above him, coiled in a Kung-Fu pose. "If you like your spleen, I'd advise you to stay down."

"Uhhhng." Ox's legs flopped around beneath him but found no traction.

"Abbey!" Mandrake seized Abbey in a hug. "You saved my life!"

Abbey squirmed beneath his squeeze. "Post a five-star review to my private crime fighter Yelp page. But please, no hugging. I hate hugging."

Mandrake eased away. "Sorry, of course. Never again."

"Abbey?" Ox said, without daring to try to raise his head. "Abbey Prue?"

"Do we know each other, delinquent?"

"We were lunch buddies. Fifth grade." Ox slicked his hair back without getting up from his prone position. "I'm Oxymandias Munoz. I used to eat your Crayons."

"Munoz? The glue-gobbler? OMG! Whatever happened to you?"

"I got held back," Ox said.

"For a decade," Billy tossed out.

Ox shot him a "do you wanna die" stare.

Abbey turned back to Mandrake. "Did the Inspector call you, too? He told me to meet here. He said he was gathering a new temporary team."

"Well, actually... " Mandrake's posture straightened. He cocked a brow, imitating the Inspector's trademark scowl. He affected a deep singsong voice. "That may have been me, my dear."

"Mandrake tricked you too." Ox cackled then whimpered. "It hurts when I laugh."

Abbey gritted her teeth and clenched her fists. "How did I fall for that?! It's horrible. It's like you're doing an Irish accent. Like that Leprechaun on the cereal box."

"I'm no Leprechaun, lassie." Mandrake continued with his horrible Irish accent.

"Please," Abbey covered her face with her hands. "Make it stop."

Ox groaned. "Let's stick him in the dumpster. Together. As a team."

"It would serve him right." Abbey straightened and dusted herself off. "But there are criminals on the loose! And I've wasted enough time." She spun and marched toward the door.

"Wait!" Mandrake chased her. "What about the team? We need you."

"Team?" Abbey stopped.

Ox waved from the ground and Billy tried to wrestle a mustard-caked sandwich wrapper from his face.

"Them?" Abbey's mouth widened and her head flung backward. She bellowed from deep within her biology.

Mandrake pleaded. "You can't save the city by yourself."

"And you think these whack-a-doodles can? Napkin face? Face-plant boy?" Abbey marched for the exit. "Thanks for the laugh."

"Am I allowed up now? Abbey?" Ox asked. "Cause I will make him drink from the urinal if you want."

Abbey shook her head and continued on her way.

Mandrake had to jog just to keep up. "You saw the studies! Detectives are at their sleuthing peak when they're kids. It's scientific fact!"

Abbey rolled her eyes. "This loser-party wouldn't last a second against Max Mandrake."

Mandrake leapt in front of her, forcing her to talk. "But the Sleuthing Seven can. And we have two of us right here. The Detective Duo."

She groaned. "Please don't repeat that."

"You complain that the Seven won't let you go out on the important missions. Well, here's your chance." Mandrake turned to Billy and Ox. "All of you are a part of it. We can save the captured detectives and the city. Together."

"I'm in if she's in," Ox said while gazing at Abbey like a lovesick puppy who just happened to beat the living lunch-money out of children.

Abbey frowned. "What's your plan, Mandrake?"

"Well, it's multi-faceted," he said.

Abbey rolled her eyes. "Start with the first facet."

Billy raised a hand and wildly waved like an overeager student with questions. "Is it team jackets? With the words "Super Secret Sleuths" printed on the back?"

"Jackets kind of defeat the 'super secret' thing," Ox said, gazing at Abbey's auburn hair. "You'd look great in a team-jacket by the way."

"We're not buying any jackets," Mandrake shouted. "That's not one of the facets!"

"Then what?" Abbey crossed her arms. "How are we going to save the Sleuthing Seven?"

"Well, step one… " Mandrake glanced down at his feet, lacking the confidence to watch their reaction to this next part. "We need a billion dollars."

When he raised his eyes, they were all staring at him, speechless, waiting for the twist.

"To buy the jackets?" Billy said. "Cause that's a lot of jackets."

"I'm out." Abbey bee-lined to the door.

Ox hurried after her. "If she's out, I'm out!"

"You're just going to give up that easy?" Mandrake yelled.

"Easy?!" Abbey stopped. Ox bumped into her. She shoved him away. "You just said we needed a billion dollars! What part of that is possibly easy?"

"Ah. That's the fun part." Mandrake smiled devilishly. "We're going to steal it. Tonight."

Abbey threw up her hands. "From who? No one in Capital City has that much money."

Mandrake smirked. This was the cool part. "I know one person who does."

Amateur Sleuthing Rule #32

Everyone has a plan until they're attacked by a chainsaw-wielding clown

"MANDRAKE!!!" A shout shattered the night air.

The middle-school sleuth sprang from the school stairs and turned toward the dark bus lane. The newly minted team had agreed to meet at the rendezvous spot after dark. Mandrake had been waiting for over twenty minutes and had begun to think this mission might be a solo one. But as he heard the fast approaching footsteps, hope coursed through him.

What he saw gave him pause — a giant bowling-pin shaped penguin waddled toward him. What form of unholy evil was this?

"It's me," the whatever-it-was grunted. "The Ox." The refrigerator sized boy sucked in his gut, and puffed out his chest. A way-too-tight tuxedo constricted his jiggly frame. "Sorry, I'm late. I was having trouble with the cummerbund."

"I can imagine." Mandrake scratched his head in disbelief. "But why?"

Ox straightened his lime green bow tie. "This is my super-secret spy uniform."

"Did you steal it from a color-blind maitre de?"

"Jealous, huh? Whatever. This looks good." Ox smoothed his lapels like a catalog model. "Where's Abbey? She's still coming right? Don't tell me I shined these patent leathers for nothing!"

"Abbey went back to the library to get something. She's late. The city is under siege. I'm worried." Mandrake sniffed. A pungent whiff of chemicals invaded his nasal cavities. He covered his mouth with his hand. "Gas!!! Gas attack!"

Ox nasally sampled the air. "No. That's my cologne. Stank. I bought it from the classy section of the drugstore. It's what all the international spies use."

Mandrake lowered the protective hand from his face. "Why would a spy wear cologne? Bad guys would smell that a mile away. Or is it meant to repel evil?"

Ox scowled. "What do you know about quality scents, Mandrake? You've got a lot to learn about the spy trade."

POOF! A bright flash blinded Mandrake. A puff of smoke followed.

The boys braced for a fight, as a caped lunatic leapt through the cloud.

"KAZAM!!!" The diminutive mystery man crash landed on the steps, causing his top hat to thunk down over his eyes.

Mandrake peered through the lingering smoke. "Billy?"

"I know not of this Billy you speak. I am the great Bill-O-Ni! Master of Magic and Mystery." He raised his hands and twinkled his fingers theatrically.

"Your cape is on fire." Ox pointed.

A bright orange flame burnt the bottom right edge of Bill-O-Ni's costume. He frantically stomped at it.

Mandrake waved away the stink of burnt polyester. "Why do you have a cape?"

"It's my detective persona. I solve mysteries using magic." Flit! A cane miraculously sprung from Billy's fingertips and doinked him in the forehead. "I'm also available for birthday parties and bar mitzvahs."

Mandrake snatched the cane away. "We are supposed to be a serious group of crime fighters. You're going to embarrass us in front of the criminals."

"Says the guy without a cape." Billy whipped the cape up to his eyes and peered out like Dracula hypnotizing a victim.

"He's right, Mandrake," Ox snickered. "You are a little underdressed for crime-fighting."

Their conversation was suddenly overpowered by the growl of an engine. Crash Brickfist's black supercharger rumbled to the curb.

Mandrake squealed gleefully. Crash was back! The Sleuthing Seven must have escaped from Crime Island. They were back on the case. This ridiculous rescue mission could be aborted!

The driver's window rolled down. Abbey stared out. She glared at Billy and Ox. "What is this? Loser Prom night?"

Mandrake gawked at the car. "Did you steal Crash Brickfist's car?"

"Borrowed. He left it parked by the library. The dude leaves his keys in the ignition. He's practically asking for it." Abbey revved the engine.

"He's gonna kill us." Mandrake slapped his forehead. "He loves that car more than he loves his hat."

"It's all good. He's a real softy for a guy with that much scar tissue." Abbey opened the passenger door. "Now get in before I get some sense and hightail it out of this town."

Mandrake and Billy climbed in the back. Ox sucked in his Yoga-Ball sized gut and limboed his way between the front seat and the dashboard as he shut the door.

Abbey winced. "What's that smell?"

"Stank." Ox fanned some fumes her way. "The scent of espionage."

Abbey cracked the window. "That cologne has a license to kill."

Ox slunked down in his seat.

Abbey kicked the car into gear and flipped on the radio. The girlie pop tunes provided an ironic soundtrack to the sights of the villain-plagued city. No one felt like dancing. They roared past the on-fire firehouse and cruised beneath the overpass strung up with wedgied cops.

Abbey flipped on a turn signal to make a left past the totem pole of stacked city buses.

"No." Mandrake pointed ahead. "Keep going straight."

"But the city jail is on Poirot Avenue."

"The Maniac Brothers blew up the jail two hours ago. All the inmates were moved."

"Moved?" Abbey said. "Where?"

Mandrake stared at the dark streets. "To the only place in the city that has enough cages to hold them."

Amateur Sleuth Rule #33

Don't torture ants with your magnifying glass

As the supercharger rumbled up to the City Zoo, its headlights caught the attention of two cops hunkered down behind a police car blocking the entrance. The cops drew their guns. One of them yelled, "Turn off the car and put your hands up!"

They trained their guns on the car and flooded its interior with flashlight beams. "If you have any weapons, throw them out of the car."

Billy reached into his mouth and threw out his retainer.

Everyone shot him a look.

Billy shrugged. "In the right hands?"

Abbey rolled down the window so Mandrake could poke his head out. "Okay boy genius, this is it. Try not to get us all shot."

The first cop, a scrawny man with a large moustache, peered inside. "Zoo's closed, kids. City's closed for that matter. Go home. Lock your doors. Don't flush your toilets."

Mandrake spied the name on the cop's gold shield: Officer McBain.

Mandrake flashed a badge. "We're on a special mission for the Mayor."

McBain inspected the badge. "Is that a Fun Sub Club Card?"

"That's on a need to know basis." Mandrake flipped his wallet shut. He leaned over and whispered. "We're undercover. We can't be carrying around real badges if we're undercover."

McBain's partner, Hunter, a curly red-haired woman with even redder lipstick, panned her flashlight across the hood of the car. "Isn't this Crash Brickfist's car?"

"We stole it!" Billy shouted.

Flashlights whisked to his face.

"Uhhh," Billy stammered. "The cats made us do it!"

"We won it." Ox slapped the dash. "In a game of Rock, Paper, Scissors. With Russian mobsters."

Now, the cops' flashlights moved to Ox.

"Don't I know you?" Hunter leaned in the window.

Ox rubbed his head, hiding his profile with his hand. "I doubt it. And if you do, I doubt you have any evidence."

Hunter sniffed. "Is that Stank?"

Ox beamed. "Why yes, it is."

"Fancy," she said approvingly.

McBain slid a finger over the sleek hard-body. "Sorry kids, we can't let you or this fine piece of machinery into zoo. Not based on a Fun Sub Club card. So beat it."

Ox snatched the keys from the ignition. "Let us in and the car is yours!" He jingled the keys in their faces like he was soothing a crying baby.

"Are you certifiably crazy?" Mandrake turned to Ox. "This is Crash Brickfist's beloved car. Have you seen Crash Brickfist? The name doesn't even do him justice"

Ox shook his head. "He'll get over it. We're trying to save his life after all."

The notion wasn't ridiculous. At least with this plan Crash would be alive to pummel someone.

Abbey snatched the keys and offered them to McBain. "Let us in and the car is yours."

Hunter stuck her face into Abbey's personal zone. "Are you trying to bribe a cop?"

"Uh." Abbey turned to Mandrake.

Mandrake hid his head in his hands.

"Too late!" Hunter snatched the car-key. "No take-backs."

The cops high-fived. McBain opened the door. "Get outs my car."

The kids climbed out. The cops rubbed their hands and cheeks all over their new black supercharger.

"I don't really like black. What do you think about yellow?" McBain said.

Mandrake closed his eyes. "Crash must never know about this."

"Hello?" Abbey waved at the cops who were now behind the wheel playing high-speed car chase. "We're on a schedule. Can you just tell us where you're holding Chief Doyle?"

Hunter lifted a ring with dozens of keys. She plucked one off and gave it to Mandrake. "He's in the lion section. Go past the monkeys, take a left at the giraffe, watch out for hyena droppings. And hyenas."

Hunter marched ahead to the main gate and used another key to unlock it. It squealed open like a haunted house door.

"You're not coming with us?" Mandrake asked.

"No way," Hunter protested. "Some of the animals got loose. Lions and bears."

"Bears?" Ox gasped. "You mean, like... panda bears? Or Koalas?"

Raaaaaawr. Something enormous growled from just beyond the zoo gates.

Everyone froze. No sudden moves.

Mandrake knees wobbled.

His courage was gone, so he faked it. He grabbed the ring of keys from McBain. "Come on team, let's rock this zoo."

He turned back to his compadres. They were hiding behind the car, quivering in terror.

AMATEUR SLEUTH RULE #34

Don't love sleuthing... love having sleuthed.

KLANG! THE COPS SLAMMED the tall metal gate shut behind them, locking them in the wild animal-infested zoo.

"Lion cage is in the back near the bears." Officer McBain wrapped a heavy chain around the iron bars. "Follow the signs past the snake house and the hardened criminals barricaded inside."

Mandrake's shoulders tightened. It dawned on him that they were trapped inside with the ferocious animals.

"Oh!" Officer Hunter shouted. "Would you mind taking his lunch to him?" She poked a greasy brown bag through the bars.

Mandrake grabbed the sack, immediately catching a 'fast-food drive through at lunchtime' scent. "Burgers?"

Hunter sighed. "Cheese Boogers was the only place open."

Mandrake chewed his lip. No doubt, every kid-eating carnivore was zeroing in on the savory chargrilled aroma.

Mandrake's knees wobbled. He tried to pawn the fast-food off to Billy.

"No thanks." Billy shrugged. "I like my limbs."

Mandrake turned to Abbey and Ox but found no sympathy as they pretended to study the nearby placard that warned about feeding the animals.

"All right. Let's make a fast-food delivery." Mandrake baby stepped forward on the concrete walkway. The others lined up at a safe distance behind him.

Grrrrrrrrr. A mysterious beast growled from a nearby bush.

Mandrake froze. "Okay, get ready to run. One. Two... "

Mandrake hurled the greasy bag high into the air and into a thicket of bushes.

A pack of four-legged creatures roared. The kids darted off in the opposite direction. They sprinted, putting some distance between themselves and the wild and hungry pack, not stopping until they reached a crossroads. Perched at the crux, a sign for "The Lion's Den" pointed toward a dirt covered path covered in a canopy of faux palm trees. A backdrop of pretend jungle sounds chirped from hidden speakers.

The group stood, not daring to move, as fleeting shadows crisscrossed the path.

"It's probably sheep." Mandrake tried to calm his pounding heart.

"Kid-eating cannibal sheep," Billy added.

Mandrake's knees shook. He took comfort in the team. Not so much that he thought they could overpower a bear, but Ox was slower than him and was a far meatier chew toy for a hungry lion. If it came down to it, he didn't have to be faster than a bear, just faster than Ox. "Let's do this quick."

Everyone nodded.

Mandrake sprinted ahead of the team with a sudden burst of energy. The adrenaline coursing through him gave him extra speed.

The group followed the bamboo signs and safari themed arrows. Hardened prisoners grouped together at the back of animal cages, called out for help, as ferocious animals pawed their cages.

Mandrake stopped at a rickety suspension bridge. Beyond it, a huge cartoonish sign shouted "MEET THE KING OF THE JUNGLE!"

Behind Mandrake, a high-pitch scream stabbed his ears. It was Abbey, the bravest, cockiest, fearless not-quite adult Mandrake knew.

This was gonna be bad.

An enormous bear lumbered onto the bridge and blocked their path, a man-sized half-eaten stuffed giraffe clutched in his jaws.

"Nobody move." Mandrake didn't need to worry. Nobody dared even breathe.

The hulking grizzly hunched down and sized them up.

"Abbey." Mandrake kept his eyes locked to the monster. "Use your karate."

"I can't," Abbey whined. "Karate only works on people. And wood."

The bear roared, spitting a splatter of phlegm, polyester batting, and faux giraffe fur into their faces.

"We should run!" Billy said. "Scream and run."

"No. Never run!" Ox gestured for them to stop.

"How do you know?" Abbey said keeping her eyes locked on the apparently hungry animal.

"After-school detention used to be held in the gym where they held the Boy Scout meetings. I spent a lot of time listening to some old guy drone on about surviving poison ivy and animal attacks." Ox's eyes went wide. "We need to scare it away."

"How?" Abbey hid behind Ox.

"In a perfect world, with a rocket launcher." Ox ducked behind Abbey.

The beast stomped forward, shaking the bridge beneath them.

"Make some noise!" Mandrake threw his hands up and did his best Sasquatch impersonation.

Billy laid down a beat-box.

Ox made fart sounds with a hand beneath his armpit.

The bear stared quizzically. Then roared deeper, angrier, louder.

"That's a challenge roar," Ox cried. "It thinks we want to fight."

The monster charged.

Billy leapt in front of the group and lifted his arms. "Kazam!" A blinding magical flash of fire and smoke exploded from his hands.

The creature stopped. Snarled. Flashed its teeth.

Billy crossed his arms, "Critics!"

"Run!" Mandrake grabbed Billy's cape and tugged him backwards.

The group sprinted off.

The bear galloped after them.

Billy barreled ahead, followed by Abbey, Mandrake taking up the rear.

But where was Ox?

Mandrake turned back to see him, about ten feet behind in the shadow of the encroaching animal.

Ox's constraining tuxedo hugged him like a mummy's bandages. Tears poured from his eyes, his arms flailed, and he wobbled like a rusted robot.

The bear leapt — a violent blur of fur, claws and teeth.

"Ox!" Mandrake yelled.

Ox slammed down on his back, his arms in the air, as the bear crashed on top of him. Saliva dripped from its wide jaws, as it bit into Ox's bow-tie constricted Adam's apple.

Suddenly, the furry monster grunted and leaned back. It shook its head. Aaaa-choo! A goop of thick bear snot splattered in Ox's face.

The grizzly began to sniff Ox's armpits, chest and neck. Again, it stiffened, blinked, then staggered backward. It slid away dizzily, its feet unsure, its balance askew. The beast wobbled drunkenly across the bridge and away from Mandrake and his team.

Ox wiped the boogery slime from his eyes, as the other kids hurried to him.

"What happened?" Mandrake studied the bear staggering away from them.

Ox lifted his black bottle of cologne. "Stank."

All of them gazed at the cologne in awe.

Mandrake snatched the bottle and doused himself liberally in the near military-grade stinkage. The others followed suit, applying a heavy dose of anti-bear cologne.

"Better stinky than sorry," Billy said before lapsing into a coughing fit.

Brimming with bulletproof confidence, they trekked off toward the lion's cage.

Amateur Sleuth Rule #35

Villains won't tell you their sinister plan while they are holding a gun on you. Villains might tell you their sinister plan if you are holding a gun on them.

THE IRON KEY SQUEALED inside the lock.

SHLANK! The cage door unlatched and creaked open.

In the dense shadows, at the center of the animal's lair, a safe distance from the edges and the dangers of snapping jaws, a creamsicle-colored human ball slumped.

The orange lump unfurled and its silvery beard glinted in the moonlight. "It's about time you came." Chief Doyle used the bars to pull himself up. "There were tigers trying to make me their midnight snack! We have to leave before they come back!"

The Chief froze as he locked Mandrake in his icy gaze.

"Hi... uh... Chief." Mandrake waved awkwardly. "Nice cage you got here."

"You... " The Chief's face burned red. "So what? You've come here to mock me? To wallow in your glory?"

"Of course not. We're here to bust you out."

Doyle cocked a brow at Mandrake's motley entourage. "Who are these degenerates? What's going on?"

"We're here on business." Mandrake decided not to flash his Sub Club Card. "The city's worst criminals escaped from Crime Island. They've taken over the City."

"Let them have it! What has this city ever done for me? Let it burn."

"You were the chief of police once!" Abbey snapped. "Show some self-respect."

"Self-respect?! I'm locked IN A ZOO!" Doyle took a threatening step forward and plopped his foot in a hot pile of lion dung. "Aaah!"

He tore off his prison issue shoe and waved it at them. "This is my life! Thanks to you, Mandrake Mandrake!"

Mandrake stood his ground. "You cared about this city once. You wanted to make a difference."

The chief laughed. "I didn't even want to be a cop. My Pop was a policeman. He made me join the force."

"What about the Mimic? You brought him down."

"You did all the work!" Doyle jabbed the shoe in Mandrake's direction. "I wanted to be a teacher. History. Roman to be specific. I loved history, books. I secretly went to night school. I was gonna finally get my degree. Instead, I'm sleeping with Orangutans!"

Mandrake closed his eyes. Recent experience had shown there wasn't much difference between heroes and villains. Maybe the chief was just one good deed away. "We all make mistakes. I didn't help the Sleuthing Seven when I should have," Mandrake pleaded. "I kept important information to myself, because I wanted fame and glory. I was jealous of everybody. I felt cheated." Mandrake blushed. This was hard to admit in front of his new friends. "Things are unfair for all of us, sometimes. Most times. But that's what being a hero is all about. Doing good, just because."

Doyle cackled like a maniac. "Just because? JUST BECAUSE?!" His bloated belly shook like a Jello mold in an earthquake.

Billy peered out into the dark zoo. "He shouldn't laugh like that! It'll draw the jackals."

Mandrake turned toward the cage door. "I'm sorry, guys. This was a stupid plan."

He stepped toward the door but Abbey grabbed his arm. She pulled him in for a whisper. "We need that stolen money. There's no other way to pay the ransom for the Sleuthing Seven."

Mandrake stared at his shoes. What more could he do? The Chief wasn't going to reveal the location of his stolen fortune to him. Mandrake wasn't a mind-reader.

Suddenly, his eyes lit up. A mind-reader! "Chief, are you familiar with Bill-O-Ni the Great?"

"The sandwich meat?" Doyle asked.

Mandrake motioned at Billy. "Bill-O-Ni is Inspector Gates' secret weapon."

"Uh." Billy wrinkled his face. "I think there's been a —"

Abbey slapped a hand over Billy's mouth and forced him to nod. "Some secret weapons are so secret, they don't even know it."

Doyle studied Billy like he was a crime scene.

"Bill-O-Ni can read minds." Mandrake pointed his fingers at his temples and did reverse cuckoo rotations.

Billy nodded emphatically, as Abbey eased her hand off his mouth. "Um, yeah. I'm a... mental... ism... er... ist."

"More like mental case," Doyle snickered.

Billy lumbered toward Doyle, stretching his out hands and twinkling his fingers like a wizard zombie.

Doyle scooted to the far corner of the cage. "What's he doing?"

"His methods are mysterious," Mandrake shrugged. "Mysterious, even to him."

Billy waved his hands in front of Doyle, like a sweaty guy airing out in front of a restroom hand dryer. He shivered, moaned, and his eyes rolled back in his head. "It's coming to me. I can taste his aura." Billy lizard-flicked his tongue.

"No! How could you?" Doyle sniffed his armpits. "It's impossible!"

"The city! He's hiding the money in the city!" Billy shouted.

"Of course." Mandrake ran with it, pointing an accusing finger at Doyle. "You know the city better than anyone."

"Get off my aura! You monster!!!" Doyle's lips quivered. "You'll never find that money."

Mandrake gave a smug smile. "You've said enough. Bill-O-Ni already has mind-sucked the hiding place."

"I have —?"

Abbey soccer kicked him in the shin.

"Ow!" Billy grabbed his leg and hopped up and down. "Ow! The pain from your thoughts is shooting down to my bruised shins."

"No! You brain-thief!" Doyle clutched his head tight. "Get out of my cage! Get out of my mind!"

Billy curtsied and handed Doyle a business card. "I also do bar mitzvahs."

Mandrake dragged Billy back to the group.

"Did you get it? Did you actually read his mind?" Abbey asked.

"Of course not. I can't do that. I can barely do card tricks," Billy whispered back.

"Doyle thinks we know. He'll lead us right to that cash." Mandrake raised his voice so Doyle could hear the next part. "Come on gang, we need to collect some stolen money."

Mandrake led the crew back into the dark zoo.

He left the large key in Doyle's cage door.

Amateur Sleuth Rule #36

A red herring is sometimes a red herring.

"This is breaking and entering," Abbey said as she followed Mandrake through the smashed-out window of the Capital City Armory.

"Actually, it's just entering." Mandrake weaved through the jagged shards that hung in the frame like the few remaining teeth of a hockey goalie, and entered the hall. "We didn't break the window. Chief Doyle did."

Mandrake's eyes adjusted to the gloom. He'd been inside the cavernous ballroom before, but the shadows cast an ominous eeriness on the otherwise drab space. Most days, the room hosted dances and weddings and festivals. But tonight, somewhere the shadows lurked a notorious bank robber.

"We were the ones who let him out of prison. While I'm no lawyer, that's worse than breaking and entering." Ox squished through the tight window, spilling into the room with a loud thud. "We'll get life in prison for that. I watch a lot of courtroom shows with my mom."

Wham! Billy fell flat on his face behind them. "It's all right! I'm okay!" He checked his nose for bleeding. "I still have my teeth."

A metallic sound rang out from an open corridor near the restroom area.

"That's the basement." Billy pointed. "Bill-O-Ni the Great did a dog's birthday party here once."

Everyone shot him a look.

"Dogs love card tricks," Billy shrugged.

Mandrake stepped ahead.

Abbey grabbed his shirt, halting him. "Are we sure about this? Following a dangerous and angry escaped convict into a dark mysterious basement seems like a bad idea."

Mandrake checked his watch. 10:25pm. They had until midnight to save the Sleuthing Seven. "I'm not sure we have a choice."

"Okay." Abbey nodded and waved him ahead. "You first."

Mandrake shuffled down the long hallway.

Abbey flipped on her flashlight, exposing paint-peeled walls and water stained ceilings. Everyone kept close. A certain Haunted House psychology settled in — no one wanted to be first, but being last was much worse.

A metal gate blocked an open utility elevator shaft. The sign affixed to it read: "Warning: Tetanus! Do not use!"

Mandrake peeked through the bars and inside the shaft. Thirty to forty feet below them, a storage elevator was parked. "He's down there."

Abbey stepped in front of the elevator buttons. "We can't just go down the elevator. It's too noisy. He'll know we're coming."

Mandrake's eyes locked on a narrow ladder affixed to the wall inside the shaft. "We'll climb down." He pulled open the heavy gate.

"That looks all kinds of dangerous," Billy spoke up. "I'm not even sure it's meant to be climbed. More like some weird elevator shaft decoration."

Mandrake pretended not to be afraid. "It's just like jungle-gym at school. No biggie."

He inched over the side, keeping his face focused away from them, not wanting to betray the wide-eyes and tightening lips that quivered in fear. His feet settled on the ladder's rungs. They were so narrow he couldn't squeeze two feet on a single bar at time.

"See, nothing to it." He held on for dear life as he carefully lowered himself one extra-careful step at a time. Nice and easy. Just like the jungle-gym... of death.

He didn't move his head, not daring to look down, and fearful looking up might throw off his balance. But as he maneuvered down he noticed the chamber was silent. Also absent was any telltale vibrations on the metal bars he desperately clung to.

He was alone on the ladder. "Guys?"

No answer came.

Mandrake snuck a peek up.

As predicted, it threw off his balance. His foot slid into the empty space below, taking the rest of his body with him.

He flailed at the rungs but the weight of his body outmatched the lack-of-strength in his muscleless arms. Before he remembered not to scream, his body plummeted downward. His panicked cry filled the echo chamber, stopping only when he smashed into the elevator's roof.

The roof caved like cardboard. He'd fallen on its trapdoor and because of its age, it crashed beneath his weight and dumped him into the interior of the elevator in a massive cloud of dust. His lungs sucked in the polluted air. A fit of coughing seized him.

A bright light blasted his face. He was caught. This moment would forever go down on his detective blooper reel, if he lived long enough to talk about it.

"Please, don't hurt me." He hacked up more dirt as he raised his hands.

"Why would we hurt you?" A familiar voice came from beyond the blinding glare.

Mandrake blinked. Behind the bright light, three figures emerged. Abbey, Ox, and the great Bill-O-Ni.

"How?"

Abbey shrugged. "There was a staircase. It was right next to the elevator. I would've called down but I didn't want to blow your cover."

Mandrake sat up. "Where's Chief Doyle?"

Abbey turned and faced an enormous graffiti-stained metal door built into the back wall — a vault. A sign on its explosion-proof steel read: "FALLOUT SHELTER".

The group moved in for a closer look.

The enormous door was open just enough for a person to slide inside.

Abbey shined her flashlight inside, exposing large piles of green.

Money! Mountains of it. Mountains and mountains. You could climb it. It filled the vault like snow filled the North Pole.

"Jackpot!" Billy clapped his hands. It wasn't the smartest move for a group trying to stay on the down-low.

Suddenly, a head burst from inside a pile of cash. "You!" Doyle yelled, squirming out from the cash. "You followed me! You couldn't read my mind. It was all trick. Wasn't it?"

Billy forced a nervous smile. "A magician never tells."

"Raaaaaaaaaaaaaaaaaah!" Doyle charged Mandrake. His hands aimed at the boy's scrawny neck.

He braced for impact —

And just as his throat was about to be throttled, Ox barreled into the heavy door, slamming it right in Doyle's face.

Doyle's face smashed against 48 inches of hardened steel. The vault latched shut with a steely KLANK.

The kids stood in silence.

"Hello?" Mandrake put his mouth up to the door. "Chief?"

"Door meets face. Door wins." Ox said.

Mandrake yanked at the handle. "It won't open!"

"That's kinda how a safe works, dude," Billy said.

Ox knocked on it. Tin-tin-tin.

Mandrake tried to squeeze his fingers between the door and the frame. "We have to break in or something."

Abbey shook her head. "There's enough nuke proof steel here to survive the apocalypse. You're not getting in. Not without the code." She nodded to a large keypad built into the vault beside the hatch.

"Why does the bomb shelter have a lock on it?" Mandrake asked.

"It's for when the zombies come," Billy said. "After the zombies attack, you don't just leave your door wide open. Duh."

"We'll just wait him out." Ox slid next to Abbey. "We could use some time to get to know each other." He pulled out a bag of dried meat and offered some to Abbey. "Jerky?"

Abbey ducked behind Mandrake. "Do something, Mandrake. Please!"

Mandrake scouted out the keypad. It resembled an extra-large phone pad with numbers and letters beneath the numbers. "We just need to figure out the password."

Billy spied over his shoulder. "I do this all the time at school for people who get locked out of their computers. Most people come up with combinations that mean something — a birthday, a pet's name."

Ox shoved them aside and punched in — D-O-G-F-A-R-T. The door didn't open. "It works on all my grandfather's computers."

KLANK! The doors behind them shut, locked. The elevator gate slammed closed.

Their heads swiveled. A large clock above the door to the safe began to tick down. Attached to it were wires, and more importantly, explosives.

"It's a bomb!" Ox shouted.

It was counting down from 59 seconds.

"Why would he have a bomb?" Billy said. "Why would he blow up his money?"

"The money's safe. It's behind a bomb shelter. It's a booby trap. To ward off people who don't know the password." Abbey said. "We have to get out of here."

Ox pulled at the knob of the door that led to the staircase. It didn't budge. "Billy! Pick the lock! Use your magic skills."

"Yeah." Billy furrowed his brow. "I kind of skipped that chapter. But I can totally turn my boogers into coins." He blew his nose and showered the floor with gold coins.

... 48 seconds...

"Everyone stay calm!" Mandrake yelled in complete panic. "What about the elevator?"

Abbey tugged at the gate. "Locked. And even if it wasn't I think you might have broken it when you cannonballed through it.

"We're gonna die." Abbey said.

... 40 seconds...

"Old folks aren't good at remembering. Usually they tape a note to the keyboard," Billy cried, looking around. "There must be something!"

Mandrake searched the room — the elevator, the graffiti-ed walls, the bomb.

Then back to the graffiti. His eyes narrowed in. Among the vulgar writings and weird names and symbols — a single word written in bright spray paint — "MIMIC"

"That's it!" Mandrake shouted. The MIMIC was the first arrest the Chief made. The one that broke his career. Mandrake rushed to the keypad and punched in M-I-M-I-C.

The door didn't open.

... 30 seconds...

"Maybe it's a code," Billy said. "MIMIC probably can be decoded to a certain numerical number. Like ASCII."

"Isn't that a computer thing?"

... 20 seconds...

"That sounds way too nerd-speak for the Chief," Abbey said. "It's not like he studied computer hacking in college... Did he?"

"No," Mandrake answered. "He was a history major... Roman

history."

"Roman history." Ox stared at the word 'MIMIC'. "Abbey, you're a genius."

"I am? I mean... I know I AM... but what genius thing did I do this time?"

... 15 seconds...

Ox pointed at the graffiti. "MIMIC isn't a word, it's a number. Roman Numerals. MIMIC is in fact the one of the few English words consisting only of Roman Numerals. And of those words, it's the highest valued number – two thousand one hundred and two. "

... 10 seconds...

Mandrake rushed to the dials.

... 5... 4...

He punched in 2-1-0-2.

BZZT. The bomb's clock went blank.

KLUNK! The door unlatched. It creaked open.

They'd done it!

Mandrake pulled the handle. It was heavy, so Ox helped him. The vault door squealed open. The Chief lay on the ground, still unconscious, at the foot of the blizzard of money. A large bruise on his forehead.

Abbey hurried inside, finding a pair of large forklifts. "We can use these to move the money up the elevator."

"And then what? How do we get it to the docks?" Billy said. "Even the toughest truck driver wouldn't drive out into the city with all those villains on the loose. Not with a truck full of cash."

"Right," Mandrake said. "We have to get people tougher than truck drivers. Bus drivers."

It was time to call in a favor.

Amateur Sleuth Rule #37

You're not a real sleuth until you have at least ten lawsuits, the press hates you, and you can't get a date.

SKREEEEEK! THE SCHOOL BUS'S BRAKES squealed as it lurched to a stop at the curb of the Capital City Armory.

"I can't believe they actually came." Abbey cruised up behind in a forklift and dumped a heap of money on a massive pile of cash. "You have more pull than I thought, Detective Brat. How'd you get them to send a bus?" Abbey stepped off the forklift.

Mandrake zipped up his coat. "Vice Principal Lestrade owed me a favor. This is it."

Mandrake moved toward the bus and flashed a warm smile as the door rattled open. "Vice Principal Lestrade, thanks for coming."

Mandrake's goofy grin collapsed like a Jenga tower. "G-g-g-grandma?"

Her pleather therapeutic shoes slid out from beneath the wheel. She wrinkled her face. Well, more wrinkled. "Get in. Now!"

Run! His brain shouted. Get away!

"NOW!" she barked.

He leapt inside, not daring defy her for another second.

Claaaank! The door slammed shut.

"Uh... Grandma... " He wanted to talk but his mind fluttered. "Where's Lestrade?" He glanced around the bus.

"He's not here," Grandma said. "I knew you'd call him. That was me you were texting, doofus. I hacked his phone."

"Hacked?" Mandrake assumed Grandma would not know what

the word meant, unless it was related to her phlegmy lungs. "This all seems very... un-Grandmotherly."

"I've been a step ahead of you this whole time." Her eyes drifted to his backpack. "I've been watching."

"Mr. Peanuts?" Mandrake felt the stuffed elephant's trunk poking through his backpack and into his shoulders. "You were the one who snuck the camera inside him? Why?"

"For your protection."

"Protection?" Mandrake gasped. "From what?"

Her bloodshot eyes peered at Billy and Ox racing forklifts through an obstacle course of car-sized mounds of loose money. "From this." She lowered her gaze back to Mandrake. "From yourself."

"Me?" Mandrake stomped. "I'm the one trying to save this city!"

Ping-Ping-Ping. Abbey knocked on the window. "Sorry to break this up. It's eleven-forty-five. In fifteen minutes, Max Mandrake's throwing his dead detective party. We need to load the bus up now or we'll never make it in time."

Mandrake closed his eyes. He needed to stay calm, professional. No time for tantrums. "Grandma, if I don't do this, people are going to die. Good people. Friends."

A growl escaped her Grandma-lipsticked pout. "If you go through with this — you and your little gang might die. Can you live with that?"

Mandrake shook his head. "You've been spying on me long enough to know. I'm good at this. Real good."

She rubbed the dark wild hair strands that sprouted from her chin. She didn't deny it.

"If those detectives die, because of what I did, and I don't even try to use my skills to save them, I'll never be able to live with myself."

Grandma removed her glasses and wiped her eyes. Mandrake had never seen her cry. Not even when she cut onions.

"I'm going back to help load the money." Mandrake turned.

CLANG! The accordion bus door straightened shut in his face.

"I know we haven't talked about it much, this unfortunateness with your father... but the two of you are on a collision course. I tried to steer you away, keep you safe all these years... but sometimes a good mother has to let her baby stick his fingers in the garbage disposal."

"I'm not sure that's right —"

"The point is — sometimes a good scolding is the only way to learn."

"Grandma, you don't —"

"Shut up and let me give you permission!"

"Okay. What? Permission?"

The bus door squeaked back open. "Load her up," Grandma said. "Did you think I'd drive down here in a bus just to ground your skinny butt?"

"No," he laughed to himself. "I guess not."

"I'm going to. So this plan had better be good. Grandma ain't got no patience for half-baked plans."

"Wait. You're coming with us?"

"You think I'm letting that girl drive a city school bus on a learner's permit?" Grandma rose to her feet. She tottered past Mandrake, down the bus steps and called out to Ox, Abbey, and Billy, who waited at the controls of their forklifts. "I'll open the back. Load up as much of the loot as you can. Nobody can count that high anyway. Bus rolls out in eight minutes."

AMATEUR SLEUTH RULE #38

Guns don't kill people,
bullets kill people.

THE SEA-WEATHERED PLANKS STRAINED beneath them like the hull of a pirate ship. The bus's tires rumbled onto the deteriorated docks and past a litany of warning signs shouting "DANGER!" and "DO NOT PASS" and "YOU WILL DIE!"

The bus's brakes squealed as the ramshackle boards buckled beneath them.

Mandrake gasped, filling his lungs with moist salty air.

The decaying Agatha Bay docks had long since been shuttered to boats and loading trucks. Ship captains preferred to use the newer ones a few miles south. Even weirdo creeps dared not step on the splintered wood.

All of this made it the perfect place for a midnight ransom drop. Provided the 'droppers' didn't sink to the bottom of the ocean with the loot.

"It's not going to hold!" Ox gophered up from the massive five foot-deep pile of money that filled the passenger section of the bus. "There's too much loot! I can't swim. I'm a sinker."

Abbey slapped a hand over Ox's mouth and dragged him back into the bills. "It's okay. I used to be a lifeguard. I'll save you."

Ox blushed. "I'm almost hoping that happens, now."

Mandrake checked his watch. 11:58. Max had set a midnight deadline. They'd made it.

Abbey nudged Mandrake. "I know plans aren't really your thing, but we might want to think something up."

"You heard of the Trojan horse?" Mandrake cocked a brow cockily. "The Greeks gave a gift of a wooden horse to the Trojans. But hidden inside were soldiers and weapons."

"But we don't have soldiers and weapons." Abbey rolled her eyes. "We've got Bill-O-Ni the Great and Stank body spray."

"Bah!" Mandrake blubbered. "I didn't want to totally rip off the Trojan horse thing. I'm no hack."

"Okay! Pipe down! This is it," Grandma hissed.

The bus lurched to a stop at the edge of the long dock. Its headlights pierced the rolling fog. Splosh-splosh. They waited in silence. The sea gently spanked the precarious structure. The rhythm was peaceful, yet ominous, like approaching war drums or the ticking of the clock before an algebra mid-term.

"It's two minutes past midnight," Billy chimed. "Maybe they came and left."

"Or maybe they smell a rat," Ox added.

"I think that's me," Billy chimed. "I should have went before we got on the bus."

"SSSSH!" Grandma librarianed them. "He'll be here. He's a greedy cuss."

Mandrake spied the sea. How was Max Mandrake going to transport so much money anyway? There wasn't a boat as far as the eye could see, no helicopter could carry this bus, and a plane would require a runway.

Mandrake turned his head toward the dock they had driven across. Maybe Max would come from behind. Maybe he'd send a truck? Except that would force his henchmen to go back through the city, compromising their location and identities. It was too mundane of a scheme for the most cunning villain on the planet.

KLANK! The earth beneath them lurched.

It wasn't the bus rolling forward. The engine was off, the parking brake applied.

"Guys! I think this dock is alive!" Billy said.

The dock had ripped away from land. Mandrake swam through the piled money like a toddler navigating a fast-food ball pit. He pressed against the back window. The floating piece of wood carved a white wake against the dark sea as they distanced themselves from the city. They picked up speed, cruising at almost 40 miles per hour.

Suddenly, the dock and the bus made a hard right turn.

"What's going on?" Abbey squeezed beside Mandrake.

"It's a submarine." Mandrake concluded. "The docks must be bolted on top of it. They're steering us out to sea."

"How could Max Mandrake get a submarine?" Billy's muffled voice squeaked from somewhere beneath the piled loot. "He's only been out of prison for a few hours."

"Maybe he's been planning this from Crime Island?" Ox's muffled voice spoke from somewhere.

"Impossible." Abbey said to the cash-pile. "He's had no contact with the outside world from Crime Island."

"He must have had help. Someone's working with him," Mandrake said. "But who?"

Suddenly, they stopped, just floating there. Mandrake's view of the front of the bus was blocked.

"HOLD ON!" Grandma hissed from the driver's seat.

KLANK! A steel claw crunched down, gripped the roof, and hoisted them into the air.

Everyone screamed.

Amateur Sleuth Rule #39

If Mrs. Scarlett did it in the Observatory with the Candlestick... step away from the board games. Nobody has Observatories anymore. And Candlesticks are so 1930.

Mandrake fought the queasiness in the pit of his stomach and scrambled for the passenger-side window. The bus drifted fifty feet in the air over the floating dock. Above them, mechanical tendrils gripped the roof and swung the bank-on-wheels over the thick steel rails of a massive container ship.

On the deck, a four man crew. One operated the crane. Two others stood beneath the dangling bus, waving it to a landing spot. The last scanned the empty sea with binoculars, paying particular attention to the sky.

Mandrake didn't need the emblazoned back patches that read "CORRECTIONAL OFFICER" to recognize the bright lime jumpsuits the crewmen wore. These were Crime Island specialists, or more likely the impostors the radio news report mentioned, who had trapped the Sleuthing Seven inside the inescapable prison.

Suddenly, the bus crashed onto the deck with a giant whomp.

Its tires hammered the deck, testing the shock absorbers. Mandrake plummeted through the cushion of loose bills to the floor of the bus. He lost sight of the others, but from the shuffling around him he assumed they were buried deep at the bottom like him. Good. Less chance of them being seen. As he climbed back to the windows, flashlights penetrated the glass and scanned the ransom.

Mandrake hoped the bounty made enough of an impression that no one would question exactly 'how much' money could fit in a school bus.

"Driver!" The crane operator had climbed down on the deck and used a mega-phone to amplify his voice. "Step out of the bus."

Mandrake recognized the voice from earlier in the library. It was Max.

"Grandma. Don't," Mandrake cried.

"I have to, boy," Grandma said, peering through the harsh light blasting her face. "Stay down."

Grandma put her hands up and wobbled out.

Mandrake crawled to the passenger side of the bus to spy the action.

"You!" Max spat through the mega-phone. "The one from the library! From the pictures!"

Grandma swatted the thing from his face. It skittered across the deck.

Max sneered. "What's your game, granny? Who are you?"

Abbey burrowed next to Mandrake. "It doesn't make sense. How does your father not know your Grandmother? She's family."

There were enough mysteries flittering around his brain that Mandrake didn't need another. "Sssh! I'm trying to listen!"

Max bent over to match Grandma's hunched posture. They faced off nose to nose.

"I'm just the bus driver," Grandma snarled.

Max circled Grandma. "I saw what you can do. You're no bus driver. Why are you living with my son?"

"Son?" Grandma folded her arms behind her back. "You're no father."

"Says the person pretending to be his mother."

"Grand-mother," Grandma emphasized.

"Interesting," Max rubbed his chin. "I've met the boy's Grandmother. Many many times. Ate her chicken pot-pie. Rubbed her swollen, calloused feet. Myrtle was her name." Max clenched his fists. "At least that's the name they wrote on her tombstone – fifteen years ago."

Mandrake jerked back. His eyes fluttered. "What... ?"

Grandma — or whoever she was — clenched her lips together. She snuck a glance back at the bus in sadness, her tearful eyes finding Mandrake's.

Max jabbed his face millimeters from her nose. "Where is my son?!"

Grandma sagged. "Somewhere far away from here. A safe place, where you'll never find him."

Max gestured to the bus. "And where did this money come from? Your social security check? Your bingo winnings? Your piggy-bank?"

His cohorts giggled.

"Does it matter?" Grandma said.

A crackle of thunder jolted everyone. But there was no storm. A sleek black helicopter majestically descended from the inky sky.

"It's the Seven," Abbey nudged Mandrake.

Hope surged through Mandrake, as he peered into the chopper's cockpit. They escaped and were here to save the day!

Max stared at it, then turned to Grandma. "Get back in the bus. Keep out of sight. Hurry!"

Grandma hesitated, perhaps weighing her options, or deciding the safest next move. But as she gazed up at the chopper, her jowls slackened, her eyes widened, and she spun back toward the bus. She rushed inside, slammed shut the door, and dove headfirst deep into the heart of the cash pile.

"Everyone stay down!" A fear in her voice. "Not a peep!"

The chopper touched down. Its blades slowed to a stop. The tinted glass shrouded the identity of the occupants.

The hatch popped and the pilot slithered a foot onto the deck of the ship. From there, Mandrake followed the pleated pants leg up to the distinct London Fog Jacket. A glint of moonlight flickered off his monocle.

"The Inspector! It's about time he showed up." Abbey began to stand but Mandrake snagged her arm.

"Wait," Mandrake whispered. "Something's not right."

The Inspector was alone. He didn't bring any reinforcements or weapons. Why get out of a bulletproof chopper to face five armed villains? He was too smart for such a rookie move.

Even more suspicious, as he strutted over, Max and his guards didn't raise their weapons, or run, or curse.

The Inspector bellowed a hearty laugh and slapped Max on the back. "I told you they'd pay, old boy. It's me after all." He gestured his hands to the sea. "This is my city! My people! I'm worth every penny to them. I'm worth a fortune."

"I don't understand?" Abbey massaged her temples. "How can they stand so close to each other without Kung-Fu punching each other in the face?"

The Inspector practically salivated as he looked at the bus full of money. "I thought we'd have to knock off Crash Brickfist before they cut a check. I figured they'd need at least a little nudge."

"You sound disappointed," Max said.

"Oh! Don't be a party-pooper, Mr. Supervillain." The Inspector scanned inside the bus.

Mandrake ducked back, burning with anger. How could this be? His hero! His role-model!

"Did you bring my payment?" Max grumbled.

The Inspector reached in his jacket and pulled out a thick bundle of papers. "Here's the manuscript. Happy reading."

Mandrake spied the cover page. It read, "FINAL DRAFT". Mandrake's eyes widened. The missing Final Draft! The mysterious contents stolen from the red envelope!

Max snatched it away and tucked it inside his coat. "And what about the rest of the Sleuthing Seven?"

"I'm afraid they're about to come to an untimely end." The Inspector checked his signature timepiece. "At 12:30 to be exact."

"But the city paid!" Max countered. "That's how a ransom works."

"You would know. But I can't take the chance that they figure this out... those sleuths were handpicked by me after all. Don't need them snooping around in our business." He tucked his timepiece away and polished his monocle with a handkerchief. "We'll name a memorial truck-stop after them. Or a turnpike."

"That wasn't part of the plan," Max growled.

"This is MY PLAN!" The Inspector jabbed a finger at Max. "Don't you forget that."

The two squared off like boxers in a grudge match. For a moment, Mandrake anticipated an epic fist fight. And given the surprising turn of events, he didn't know which side to root for. Maybe a tie was best, where they both ended up in the hospital.

"Get off my BOAT!" The Inspector spat.

Max clenched his jaw and balled his fists then turned and marched to the edge of the boat.

Abbey nudged Mandrake. "What's going on?"

Mandrake knew, but wasn't yet ready to voice the truth — Inspector Gunther Gates had gone villain.

A moment later, Mandrake glimpsed the dock they floated in on, drifting away, with Max presumably tucked beneath it inside the submarine.

The Inspector clapped his hands twice. "Let's get this boat to a bank!"

"What do we do now?" Billy whispered.

Mandrake wished he knew. He'd planned to stop Max, but not his mentor, his role model, the leader of the Sleuthing Seven. He was too emotional to come up with any smart scheme. His only hope was that Abbey had a —

"Inspector!" Abbey boomed as she stepped off the bus.

The Inspector appraised her with stunned eyes. His henchman aimed their weapons.

"It's me." Abbey put her hands up. "Abbey Prue."

Mandrake scrambled for the door, but Grandma grabbed his ankle. She shook her head and mouthed, "Not yet."

She was right of course. What was he going to do against a gang of armed baddies? Still, leaving Abbey out there, all alone, felt wrong.

She inched toward the Inspector. "So, I assume this is some sort of sting operation. You're trying to throw Max off the track, so you can free the Sleuthing Seven, right?"

"Got me!" The Inspector shot her with some mimed gun fingers. "That's why you were always my favorite. I handpicked you for the team, you know? Pinot wanted that clue-sniffing Dane. But not me. Plus, I'm allergic to dogs."

"What was in that envelope you handed Max Mandrake?" Abbey put her hands on her hips. "A GPS tracker? A wire-tap?"

"I can't tell you all my secrets. Someone might be listening." The Inspector nodded to the bus. "Who else is hiding in there? Surely, you didn't come alone."

The Guards turned their guns to the bus.

Abbey backpedaled. "No! I came on my own. I swear. You know me – I'm a solo operator. There's no 'Me' in 'Team'."

"No, no there isn't." The Inspector pulled his Luger pistol from his jacket. "That makes things much cleaner."

The color drained from Abbey's face. She closed her eyes.

"Wait!" Mandrake burst out of the bus, climbed out, and put himself between the Inspector's gun and Abbey. "You don't want to do that!"

The Inspector notched a brow. "And why not?"

"Because you're on TV." Mandrake waved to the air. "It's all being live streamed. Right now."

The guards trained their aim on the boy detective.

Abbey gave Mandrake a sideways glance. "Mandrake, what are you doing?"

"Improvising," Mandrake whispered. He slid his glasses up his nose and raised his voice theatrically. "I have a spy-camera built into my glasses."

The Inspector studied Mandrake's thick lenses. "Is this a network thing? Or Internet-only?"

"Both. And now the world knows what you've done. How else could those crooks have escaped from an inescapable prison?" Mandrake pointed an accusing finger at the Inspector. "You designed it after all, you knew the weak spots. You created them."

"Ridiculous." The Inspector twisted sideways. "Be sure to get my profile in the shot. This is my good side."

Mandrake paced in front of the Inspector. "The briefcase you brought the night of Max Mandrake's escape... the night you disappeared. I'm guessing that was where you hid the Inspector disguise Max wore when he pretended to be you and walked out of the prison."

A nervous chuckle escaped from the Inspector's lips. "You've got quite an imagination, young man."

"I saw him in costume at the library earlier today. He looked identical. Except for the monocle."

"Even if this ludicrous scheme happened the way you say, where did I go?" The Inspector leaned close, going nose to nose. "Into thin air?"

Mandrake caught a whiff of something, a scent of smoke and apricot. Mandrake remembered the Inspector's favorite pipe blend. "You must have been there. Somewhere?"

"Preposterous!" The Inspector punched the air. "Why would I help my greatest nemesis?"

Mandrake wasn't sure. But Crash had taught him that if you confidently laid some dots out for the suspect to connect, they could do most of the work for you. "Well... books!"

"Books?" The Inspector said. "I had a bestseller."

"Not recently," Mandrake said. "Not since Max Mandrake went to prison."

"That's ridiculous." The Inspector let out a nervous laugh. "My books do fine."

"They do fine gathering dust beneath the library. Face it, Inspector. With all the Master Criminals in prison, it left you with little to do... your memoir's sequel bombed, your TV pilot failed. You're a has-been."

The Inspector waved his gun at Mandrake. "I saved this city! More times than I can count."

"And yet no one cares."

"They need to be reminded! The only reason anyone is safe is because of me."

Mandrake crossed his arms. "And how better to remind everyone of that then to unleash the greatest criminals in the world on a defenseless city?"

The Inspector snatched the glasses off Mandrake's face and threw them to the deck. And stomped them.

Mandrake's world went blurry.

"You're a bright little one. But you're as reckless as your father." The tall, unfocused blob in front of him said.

"You can't just kill your friends," Abbey chimed.

"Friends? You mean — Crash? Pinot? The Twins?" The Inspector threw his head back and cackled. "Losers! Detecting isn't a team-sport, little girl. The lot of them have been dragging me down for years."

Mandrake's feet fished around for his smashed spectacles as he talked."But you have the ransom! You made a deal!"

"Max Mandrake made that deal!"

Mandrake felt a slight crunch beneath the balls of his feet. He reached down and lifted the broken glasses to his eyes. "You purposefully made the money too much! You knew they wouldn't pay."

"I knew they couldn't." The Inspector flashed his eyes at the bus. "I thought one billion would be too much money for them to collect on short notice. It's too late now. The timers are set."

"Timers?" Mandrake glared at him through a spider web of prescription glass. "You set a bomb at the prison?"

The Inspector hissed a cloud of pipe-smoke. "You think I'm going to give up my whole plan?"

"That's why you pulled your guards out. That's why you've left Crime Island unguarded. Because you're going to destroy it. With a time bomb."

"Clever boy. You figured me out." The Inspector tapped his timepiece. "But at exactly thirty minutes past midnight, there won't be anyone left to bring me to justice."

"What about us?" Abbey said. "We'll still be here."

"Optimism. How adorable," The Inspector said. "But I'm afraid you'll be gone too."

"Not if I have anything to say about it." Knuckles cracked near the front of the bus. Mandrake knew those knuckles. Ox stepped out beside Abbey.

BOOM! A smoke bomb went off. Billy leapt through the hazy cloud. "The Great Bill-O-Ni in the hizzy!"

The Inspector waved his Luger at them. "What is this? The junior league?"

"No," Ox corrected him. "We're just the distraction."

"The distraction? From whaaaaa—?"

An engine roared to life. Everyone turned to see the bus kicking into gear. The Inspector was caught in its path. BAM! The bus slammed into him flipped the detective up on its hood.

The Inspector raised his head and dizzily stared through the windshield. "YOU!"

Grandma was in the driver's seat. She hit the gas, as the guards screamed and dove for cover.

The bus smashed through the steel railing and rocketed off the side.

SPLOOOOSH! The yellow vehicle plunged bumper-first into the ocean, sending an explosion of water over the deck.

"Nooooooo!" Mandrake screamed.

The bus sunk out of view and into the deepest depths of the sea.

Amateur Sleuth Rule #40

Always follow the money... unless it's into a bees nest or an active volcano or a minefield.

Mandrake ran to the edge of the ship and leapt off the side.

He was snagged in mid-air.

Something had him by the belt.

Something Stanky.

Ox yanked him backward and the two of them crashed onto the deck.

"Sorry Mandrake," Ox said. "The Sleuthing Seven's lives ain't gonna save themselves. They need you to rescue them. If you drowned, it would make that hard."

Running feet thundered past them. The guards raced to the edge and looked over the side.

"The money!" One of them yelled as he tore off his boots. "Save the money!"

The guards tossed away their weapons, ripped off their clothes and dove into the dark sea after the sinking bus.

Mandrake wasn't worried about the cash. He had but one concern. Tears wet his eyes as he lumbered toward the obliterated rail.

"Grandma... "

A burble of white foam marked the spot where the school bus had punched through the dark sea. The guards desperately swam around the spot, searching for bundles of cash that might float back to the surface. But there was no hint of money and no sign of the sunken bus.

Mandrake stared down in horror. He imagined his Grandma

chauffeuring a billion dollars straight to the bottom of the dark sea.

Abbey put a hand on Mandrake's shoulder. "I'm so sorry. She saved our lives."

Grandma had warned him not to come here, not to play hero like he was some great savior of the city. She was so right. He'd been wrong about everything. He set out to bring down his father, to settle a score — when the real danger was the man he aspired to be.

"She told us to distract them," Billy said. "I didn't know she planned to drive off the side."

Abbey stared down at the water treading guards. "She knew the guards would jump in after the money. She knew exactly what she was doing."

Mandrake closed his eyes, flushing a stream of tears down his cheeks. He pictured her sweet wrinkled face. The way it turned rosy when he told her he loved her. The way it felt when she hugged him goodnight and when her soft crackly voice whispered —

"Hurry up, boy! I can't hang here all day!"

It sounded so real. Like she was there.

"Open your eyes, boy!!!" The voice grunted from the side of the boat.

Mandrake raced to the obliterated rail. "Grandma?!"

She hung off a lifeboat. Her feet dangled above the inky sea.

She was alive!

Abbey pulled a lever, activating a mechanism that raised the lifeboat up.

Grandma spilled onto the deck. The kids gathered around her.

Mandrake's jaw hung open. "Grandma, how?"

"I jumped before the bus went in the water." She grumbled. "What? Do you think I'd just drive a bus over the side of a ship without a plan?"

"Well, some of us are a little plan-challenged." Abbey nudged Mandrake.

"I thought I'd lost you!" Mandrake threw his arms around the old woman. Abbey tapped Mandrake on the shoulder. "Guys. I hate to break this up, but if the Inspector set the bombs for twelve-thirty, we only have like five minutes."

"What can we do?" Billy threw his hands up. "We'll never make it there in a boat."

Mandrake stared past them to the helicopter. "We're not taking the boat."

AMATEUR SLEUTH RULE #41

If you don't know whether to cut the red or the blue wire, run!!!!

ABBEY PILOTED THE HELICOPTER into a wall of dense fog. Somewhere in the muck, high-above the raging ocean, the hanging concrete bunker known as Crime Island lurked. They had moments before it would explode, along with six of the world's greatest detectives.

"Ox, flip on the spotlights," Abbey instructed Ox who was smooshed into the co-pilot's seat.

He flipped a switch on the control panel. KLACK! Powerful lamps shined beams of light forward, cutting through the dense night gray haze...

"I suppose it would be silly of me to think you had some awesome plan," Abbey called to the backseat.

Mandrake, who was squeezed between Grandma and Billy, wriggled forward. "I have parts of a plan. It's plan-ish at least. First, we find the bomb, then we defuse it."

«'Defused' is actually a Hollywood term," Ox said. "A bomb is never 'defused'... but it can be disarmed. I did a science project on exploding stuff three years ago. Came in third. Before the accident."

"You know how to defuse a bomb?" Abbey asked.

"I've watched YouTube videos."

Billy plugged his ears with his fingers. It wasn't the biggest vote of confidence.

"Gates could have hidden the explosives anywhere," Grandma grumbled. "Even if we could defuse it, it's a needle in a haystack."

"It's 12:28. Haystack goes kaboom in two minutes, fyi," Billy peered at his watch.

"We don't have time to search the whole prison," Abbey said.

"I'll go inside and get the detectives out." Grandma hastily unbuckled her seatbelt.

Mandrake grabbed her arm. "In four minutes? Just getting through the Frisk-o-Matic would take five."

"What in tarnation is a Frisk-O-Matic?" Grandma asked.

"It's a machine that prevents lethal weapons from getting inside the prison." Mandrake froze, realizing what he said. "Lethal weapons. Like...bombs. The explosives can't be inside the prison! They'd never make it past the Frisk-O-Matic!"

Ahead, the blinding searchlights of the four tall support towers poked through the thick haze.

Ox shielded his eyes with his hands. "If the bomb is on the outside, we can find it!"

The rotors whined as Abbey dipped the chopper toward the rectangular incarceration building that hung from the towers like a strip-mall on a swing. Crime Island resembled a smooth brick. The only blemish on its unobstructed surface was the painted helipad and the single steel hatchway entrance. From what Mandrake's inspection, there wasn't a bomb or explosive on it.

"It doesn't make sense," Abbey hovered the helicopter mere feet above the top of the prison, close to the hatch that served as its only entrance. "Crime Island is built like a bunker. They didn't want anyone breaking in or out. It can survive a nuclear blast. A bomb on the outside wouldn't even dent it."

Mandrake nodded. Finding a bomb wasn't any different than figuring out who robbed a bank or how someone broke into a museum.

He needed to think like a villain!

What would the Inspector do? Or Max?

If they couldn't get the bomb inside, how would they destroy it?

Mandrake scanned the surrounding area — the prison, the raging sea beneath it, the towers, and the cables.

The cables! Of course! They were the weak spots! "The guard tower! Where the cables connect! That's where the bombs are!"

The rotors groaned as Abbey veered upward.

Mandrake pointed to the tiniest of green lights in the distance. "He can't blow it up, but if he takes out the cables he can send the entire thing plummeting downward. The fall will destroy the building and what's left will be washed into the ocean."

The chopper zoomed toward the tower. The explosive device came into view, a bundle of wires and dynamite all topped off with a digital display, presumably the detonation controls.

«Two minutes!» Billy held up his watch.

Ox cracked his neck, tough-guy style. "Put me on the cable, I'll do the rest."

Abbey turned to Ox. "You don't have to do this to impress me."

Ox grinned. "I've done some bad things in my life. One time I put super glue on every toilet in the faculty bathroom. They had to call the fire department to pry people off. But this night has changed me. I want to be different. I can do things. Useful things. I want to use my bully powers for good, to have real friends, to know what it feels like to go home right after school and not go to detention, to eat my own lunch for a change."

Abbey gave Ox a smile. "You might actually have potential, Oxymandias."

"I might? Really?!" Ox beamed. "Cool. Very cool."

"Ninety seconds," Billy yelled.

Ox went for the door.

"Stop!" Grandma yanked Ox back into his seat and climbed over Billy to the door of the chopper. "Sorry kid, but if anybody is going out on that wire to defuse a bomb it's going to be me."

Grandma kicked open the chopper door and —

KAA-BOOOOOOM! The dynamite detonated! A flash of fire blinded them. Grandma toppled backward, on top of Billy as burning shrapnel peppered the helicopter's bulletproof windows. The group held on tight as the chopper dropped and swerved.

"Whoops," Billy tapped his wristwatch. "My watch was off by exactly one minute."

Metal shrieked as the explosion sheared one of the thick support cables. The remaining three tower-cables buckled under Crime Island's colossal weight.

The hanging prison lurched and strained, but didn't collapse. Yet.

Mandrake knew Crime Prison only had precious minutes before the other support cables ripped away and the whole thing crashed into the raging sea hundreds of feet below. "We have to go in."

Amateur Sleuth Rule #42

When defusing a bomb, if you don't know whether to cut the red wire or the blue — hold your ears, things are about to get very very loud.

The hanging prison twisted and turned like a swing in a hurricane.

Abbey feathered the chopper's controls with the care of someone putting a roof on a house of cards. Every time she tried to land, the structure swayed out from under her.

"I'm not going to be able to put her down," Abbey said.

"Just get us close." Mandrake studied the three remaining steel cables, which were unraveling fast. "We've got ten minutes at best."

Abbey frowned. "I'll stay by the hatch. As soon as you come out I'll come for you."

Mandrake nodded.

"I can't let you do this." Grandma held the chopper door shut.

"Abbey has to fly the chopper, and I'm the only other one who has been inside that place."

Abbey hovered the skids inches above the shuddering prison roof.

"There's no time to argue. So I'll just say, sorry." Mandrake winked at Billy, who nodded conspiratorially and shoved the chopper door open.

Grandma lunged for Mandrake but her arm caught on something. Billy! He'd handcuffed her wrist to his.

"Abracadabra?" Billy shrugged.

Grandma's face burned red.

"Don't kill Billy. This is what's right." Mandrake leapt out onto the wobbly concrete. The roof floated beneath him like a strip-mall-sized skateboard. He stiffly ambled toward the open steel hatch as his sea legs adjusted to the motion.

Mandrake dipped his foot inside when —

A hand snagged his collar! Grandma! She and Billy stood behind him. "Sorry, M." Billy raised his arm showing the still attached handcuff. "There's some thunder in those flabby old lady arms."

Grandma yanked Billy's chicken wing arm back down. "Mandrake Mandrake Mandrake! Get back in that helicopter this instant!"

"Your middle name is Mandrake too?" Billy asked.

Mandrake glanced back at the helicopter, which now circled fifty feet above the prison. "Grandma, Abbey's not coming back until the detectives are out of the prison."

Grandma marched to the hatch, dragging Billy with her. "Take these off me!"

Billy shrugged. "Actually, I can't. I couldn't afford the trick cuffs. And the real ones were cheaper without the keys."

Grandma snarled. "We'll make this quick! Climb on my back!"

She knelt down and Billy straddled her shoulders piggy-back style. Grandma launched through the metal hatch and ignored the ladder's rungs, choosing to slide down fireman-pole-style straight to the bottom.

Mandrake scrambled down after them, joining them in the prison's solid steel security room. Surprisingly, it didn't look much different than the last time he'd encountered it. No sign of any struggle or fight. Whatever happened here went down tidily.

Mandrake weaved around the mini-golf like holes in the floor and tapped the wall-sized touch screen computer. It flashed on and he quickly navigated its menu screens to initiate the Frisk-O-Matic.

The weapons tray spit from the wall. Mandrake brought it over to Billy and Grandma

"If you're hiding any weapons, put them in here. No weapons." Billy glanced down at his magic suit. "Just sponge balls. And a rabbit."

Grandma dug inside her frilly dress and retrieved four deadly throwing knives. She dropped them into the tray.

Mandrake stared judgmentally. "Grandma!"

She wasn't done. With her non-cuffed hand, she dug inside the waist of her flowery fabric and removed a small arsenal — nun-chucks, brass knuckles, a mace, a blowgun, a sling-shot.

"Anything else?" Mandrake lifted the tray to her face.

She kept going. A derringer, four Ninja stars, a short sword, two hand-grenades, and another blowgun tucked into her therapy stockings.

Mandrake hurried the weapons-filled tray back to the wall.

A robotic voice chirped from the speaker above them. "Assume the position!"

Everyone planted their feet in the large cartoon-ey footprints set in the floor. Mechanical arms sprung from the holes around them. Steel fingers began to poke and prod their bodies.

The urge to laugh boiled within Mandrake. Hold it together, he told himself. Things were dire. The prison was about to collapse. Laughing in the face of death was one thing, giggling to the point of peeing was quite another.

A surprising noise came from his right — "Bwahahahaha!" It was Grandma. She cackled. Out of control. "Bwahahahahahaha!"

"Muhahahahahahaha," Billy added.

Mandrake went with it. "Hahahahahahahaha-hooohoooohoohoo."

The building lurched ominously. The steel around them to shrieked and squealed.

"The second cable just broke!" Billy hooted. "We're doomed!"

"Whoooohahaha! We need to hurry." Grandma whooped helplessly from the robotic hand maneuvering up her back. "Or die!

Wahahaahaha!"

Finally, the frisk-bots retracted and the computer powered off.

"Frisk-o-Matic complete," the computer voice droned. "Thank you."

The room sunk, elevator-like, lowering them to the first level of the prison. Clunk. The floor settled at the entrance to the Warden's control room with a pneumatic hiss.

Mandrake raced to the control room. Grandma followed, which meant so did Billy.

Static filled the boxy wall-mounted televisions. The violent quaking must have knocked a wire loose.

Mandrake hit the large red button. The caged door to the prison hallway opened. "Follow me!" He shouted and led them through. The door hammered shut behind them.

Grandma stopped and pulled at its bars. "We're locked in."

"That's gonna be a problem," Billy said. "Especially given the whole thing is about to collapse."

"We'll figure it out later," Mandrake said. "First we need to find the Seven."

He sprinted down the long corridor. The prison cells that lined the walls were open and empty. The impenetrable glass window-walls had retracted out of view into the ceiling and floors. There was no sign of anyone. The place felt even creepier without the super villains locked up inside. The last cell at the far end — the one directly across from Max's — was still sealed shut.

Mandrake stepped toward it.

Suddenly, Crime Island tilted downward. Grandma, Billy and Mandrake toppled across the floor, crashing into the wall at the end of the hall.

"Kid?" A voice with more gravel than a cement mixer called from the caged cell behind him.

"Crash?!" Mandrake turned to see Crash, Pinot, the Farleys, and Professor Lung all squeezed onto a single prison-issued bed like some cartoon family on an undersized couch.

The legendary detectives stood and rushed to the glass that encaged them.

"Zuts alors! Mandrake Mandrake." Monsieur Pinot turned his eyes to Billy and Grandma. "And friends!"

"This is our rescue team?" The shell-shocked Warden pushed through the glut of detectives and squashed his face against the thick glass. "We're doomed."

Billy knocked on the glass. "How do we get you out?"

"The cells can only be opened from the control room," the Warden said.

"The one that locked behind us when we came in?" Billy nodded back to where they entered from.

The Warden burst into tears.

Mandrake shrugged . "Woopsie."

Billy scratched his head, dragging Grandma's hand with his. "If it only opens from the outside, how did you end up here?"

"I don't know." The Warden could barely talk through his sobbing. "The door to the prison hallway popped open on its own. It's not supposed to do that. The bad-guys grabbed me and threw me in here. Now I'm going to die."

"What about the Inspector?" Professor Lung asked. "He's here somewhere. He built this wretched place! He'd know how to get out."

Mandrake raised a brow. "Don't you know?"

"Know what? He sent us here," Farley said, "to investigate this cell. Once we entered... the other prison cells opened and the bad-guys locked us in with the Warden."

Mandrake frowned. One last fail-safe on the Inspector's part. If his scheme didn't work, he could blame everything on Max Mandrake and the other super-crooks.

The entire prison lurched and quaked. The Detectives grabbed the walls to keep from falling.

"The Inspector built this place. There must be an override hidden inside the prison!" Mandrake turned to the open cell opposite the detectives. Max's prison cell. It was wide open but still held all of Max's personal effects — mostly a bunch of finger-painted 3D masterpieces that hung on the walls.

Grandma pulled Billy behind Mandrake. She gazed at the painting of the teary-eyed Mindy Mandrake. Despite the violent shaking and ominous reminders of their impending doom, it commanded her attention.

Mandrake gazed at Grandma. Her lower lip quivered. Her eyes were wet. She wiped them, trying to hide the emotion.

It was too hard to see her like this. Mandrake turned to the portrait that filled Grandma with so much sadness. Mindy and those sad, sad eyes. And then he realized — the eyes were the same – Grandma's and Mindy's. Identical!

Billy nudged Mandrake. "You might want to hurry up with the whole rescue mission. I'd prefer not to die. I've got tons of stuff on my DVR."

"On it!" Mandrake slid inside Max's cell, taking in every nook and cranny. "There's something different." Visually, nothing had changed inside Max's old residence — not the paintings, not the paints, or even the bed. He approached the taped Rules of Amateur Sleuthing and tore them down.

"You're the only one who can do this." Grandma put her free hand on Mandrake's shoulder. "You have the Nose."

Goosebumps raised on Mandrake's arms. The Nose. Of course — that was it! Not the Nose, but his nose.

There was something different about the Max's prison cell.

"Apricot Fire!" Mandrake remembered the Inspector's signature brand of pipe tobacco and realized it was the scent he detected the last time he was here. More importantly, it was now gone. "He was here! Hiding. But where?"

Mandrake hurried to the back wall. His eyes widened. He reared back, and punched the concrete.

Riiiip! His fist slammed through the wall like he was punching paper. Because it was paper! A canvas! A 3D illusion of reality, just like the smaller paintings Max displayed around the room. Mandrake ripped through, revealing a small hiding space.

"He didn't vanish!" Billy said. "He was just hiding all along."

Mandrake nodded. The inspector must have been sitting here, smoking his trademark pipe and signature Apricot Fire tobacco, while he plotted the next phase of his devious scheme. "There must be a secret control panel in this wall."

Grandma tapped her knuckles on the real wall. With each knock came a solid THUNK.

Mandrake followed her lead. "A secret wall panel would have to have been built into the prison from the beginning."

THUNK. THUNK. THUNK.

"I don't understand!" Frank Farley scratched his head. "The Inspector designed this prison. Why would he design that?"

Thud! A hollow sound greeted Mandrake's knuckles. This was it!

"Back up," Grandma said.

They did. Well, Billy did his best given the handcuffs. Grandma karate-kicked the suspicious spot. It caved in beneath her strike.

Mandrake dug his fingers into the broken piece of wall and peeled away the kick-dented plaster, revealing a control panel, identical to the Warden's!

"The Inspector may have some explaining to do," Father O'Malley said.

Mandrake pressed a button.

"OVERRIDE ENGAGED," came the sing-song computer voice.

In the cell across from Mandrake, the glass wall trapping the Sleuthing Seven slid away, followed by a loud THWACK from the hall, which signaled the disengagement of the main door's lock.

This was going to work! They were going to survive!

A deafening CRAAAAAACK shook the prison.

And the world literally turned upside down.

AMATEUR SLEUTH RULE #43

Contrary to popular belief, the fall won't kill you. But you will feel the concrete.

THE ENTIRE PRISON SWUNG beneath the last remaining cable. The roof hatch popped open and the detectives' heads poked out. It wasn't really the roof anymore. The prison hung at ninety-degree angle. It was more like they were sticking their heads out of the window of a skyscraper and staring straight up its face to the sky above.

Mandrake waved to Abbey. The chopper veered to them and hovered in front of them. She kept a safe distance, not willing to risk getting hit by the massive building swaying in the air. The only possible landing zone was what used to be the east side of the prison. It now hung above them, serving as the roof about thirty yards up.

The enormous weight of prison was too much for just two fracturing steel cables. The final cable began to shred, its metallic threads fraying strand by strand...

"We have to climb!" Grandma pointed to one of the already severed cables, which limply dangled just outside the hatch. "Now!"

Like a line of hungry ants the group grabbed hold of the sheared cable and scrambled up the steep swaying concrete.

Crash tucked Mandrake on his massive back and scaled ahead. It wasn't surprising the burly Crash Brickfist could pull himself up the steep prison cliff. But all of the Seven displayed expert climbing skills. No matter their age, shape, or size, an adventurer's heart beat in every one of the detectives.

Grandma brought up the rear still dragging the handcuffed Billy along while also helping the husky Warden.

The heroes crawled out onto what was now the new top of the structure.

Abbey hovered the chopper in front of them, careful not to land on the teetering prison.

They began piling inside. First the Farleys, then Pinot, O'Malley, and Lung. It was a tight squeeze. The cabin was only built for four passengers. They sat on top of one another, packing it like some Clown Car.

Soon the cabin was overstuffed with bodies, leaving no room for Crash, Mandrake, Grandma and Billy.

"Looks like we ride on the outside, gang." Crash said.

Grandma nodded. "It's okay. Hold tight."

They hopped onto the chopper's skids and clutched its exterior handrails. Crash slapped the chopper's window, signaling Abbey.

She pulled back the stick. The helicopter wobbled, then sputtered, then crashed down on top of the prison. Everyone jolted from the impact.

The support cable strained. The prison hung by a single strand.

They were seconds away from catastrophe.

The chopper wheezed but couldn't lift off of the roof.

Abbey called out: "It's too much weight."

"Looks like this is goodbye, kid." Crash let go of the handrail.

Mandrake grabbed his arm. "You won't survive, Crash."

Crash took off his hat. "You're scaring me kid — you're the one who's supposed to believe the impossible is possible."

Mandrake's lungs tightened. "I'm sorry, for what I said before."

Crash handed him his hat. "Don't sweat it, kid. It's where we end up that matters, not how we get there."

Mandrake hugged the big lug. Crash wasn't much of a hugger but under the circumstances, he went with it.

"Get this handcuff off of me," Grandma pulled a bobby-pin from her bluish bun and handed it to Mandrake. "I know you can pick the stupid lock. I've watched you do it in your room. Mr. Peanuts, remember."

"But – "

"DO IT!" She insisted.

Mandrake wiggled the pin inside the lock. "Mom... "

She couldn't have been surprised he'd figured it out. She knew his detective prowess. She must have known he'd solve her mystery one day.

Clack. The metal bracelet sprung open. She was free.

"I wanted to tell you, more than anything." Tears pooled at her eyes. Her voice softened, no longer the gravely grunts, or old lady-speak. She spoke with the velvety smooth sound of a trained Hollywood actress.

The prison shook violently beneath the failing cable.

"It's over three hundred feet... the highest you've dove from is one-fifty."

"It'll be a new world record," she smiled. "Cool."

"Wait." Mandrake touched the button on her white home-alert bracelet. It wasn't what it looked like. It triggered the morph-technology. Grandma's fake skin rippled and bubbled. The 80-year old face melted away, replaced by the stunning features of Mindy Mandrake.

They stared at each other, mother and son, for the first time... despite the world collapsing around them. There was so much to say. Too much.

Crash Brickfist watched in stunned silence, as did the others.

Without taking her eyes off her son, Mindy spoke to Crash, "Take care of my boy, Brickfist... "

She skipped off the chopper.

Now unburdened, the aircraft lifted off the concrete.

Mindy's motherly eyes stayed on Mandrake. "I'm sorry I lied. I'm sorry about Poodle Springs. And I'm really sorry about giving you that silly name. That was your father's idea."

Mandrake blushed. "Truth is... I kind of like the name."

Mindy yelled over the whine of the rotors. "I couldn't be prouder of you."

The chopper drifted away, as Mandrake basked in her radiant glow. For a brief micro-second their impending doom didn't matter. "I'm proud of you too, Mom."

SNAAAAAAAAAAAAP! The last bit of the cable ripped.

The prison plummeted downward into the ocean as the helicopter zoomed toward the sky. Mindy launched herself off the side of the building. Perfect form, hands out, great trajectory, majestic even, a spectacle marred only by the enormous concrete bunker crashing to the sea beside her.

There was beauty to it, and tragedy.

Then there was violence.

KA-SPLOOOOSH! The prison smashed into the ocean in an explosion of water. Mandrake turned his head. Instinct told him not to watch, not to implant this tragic image deep into the personal photo-gallery of his soul.

Instead, he'd remember her floating gracefully like an angel.

His angel.

He knew it was impossible to survive a free-dive from three hundred feet.

But as the chopper gently drifted away, he took solace in entry #47 of the Rules of Amateur Sleuthing— "A good detective always refuses to accept the impossible!"

Amateur Sleuth Rule #44

If you haven't checked their pulse, they're not dead.

The usual living room light glowed through the front window of Mandrake's grandmother's house. What was unusual — other than the fact everything was different now — was the overcoat-cloaked figure that stalked the driveway.

Crickets masked the stranger's footsteps as he crept to the porch. The whites of his eyes pierced the gloom cast from the fedora that veiled his face. He spied Grandma, who sat in her favorite chair, knitting away. Her focus was entirely on the blue-whatever-it-was that rested on her lap. A sweater? A blanket? A doily? Who knows? Maybe she didn't.

His gloved hands held a bent wire, which he used to pick the lock of the front door. He slipped silently into the foyer, his black boots cushioned by the tacky shag, leaving only the klik-klak of the knitting needles.

"I have a rule about hats in the house," Grandma said, not bothering to look up.

The stranger removed his hat, revealing the all-too-familiar face of Max Mandrake.

Grandma stole a sip of tea. "I was wondering when you'd show up... "

"Mindy... all these years I thought you were dead... how could you do this to me?"

Grandma gently placed her tea-cup back on its coaster. "Mindy... I'm afraid not."

"I know about everything." The master villain held up the envelope the Inspector handed him on the freight the night Crime Island collapsed.

"Ah," Grandma twitched. "That's what all of this hullabaloo was about? I wouldn't believe everything you read."

"I didn't believe any of it at first, but when the Inspector showed me he had access to the Max-a-Morph, I knew there was only one person who could have given up my own invention."

"So what's this?" Grandma gestured to the packet Max waved in the air. "The Inspector's dear diary?"

"It's his next book. A preview. Telling the truth of what happened that night. What he did, what you did." Max slammed the envelope down on the coffee table, rattling the lamp.

Grandma put her knitting down. "Give me the quick version. The headlines."

"You know the story — the bridge, the Inspector, the deal."

"A deal? Between adversaries. Imagine that." Grandma snickered.

"I should have realized it was you the second I saw your bracelet." Max threw a glance at the home alert gizmo around her wrist.

"I'm a good actress."

"The best. But this is insanity. Being forced to live your life as this decrepit thing."

"I like to think of myself as a fine wine or an old cheese."

"If you wanted out, you could've come to me," the dark intruder shouted. "I would've protected you. Given you whatever life you wanted!"

"I'm not sure I understand," Grandma said.

"I know all about it. You gave me up to Gates!"

"I'm just an old woman."

"Give it up, Mindy. I know all about your trick! The blanks. The candy-glass windshield. Your dive off the bridge."

"They found Mindy's body —"

"They found a body. Not Mindy's. Some poor Jane Doe the Inspector stole from the morgue. But this... living your life as an old lady. Using my technology. You always wanted to be an actress."

"My greatest role." The old woman folded her hands.

"Sworn to secrecy no doubt," the man said. "If anyone knew, you'd go to prison and so would Inspector Gates."

Grandma raised her eyebrows.

Max slammed his fist in his hand. "You could've sent me a message."

"And ruin the surprise?"

"You ruined us!" The super criminal took a threatening step toward her.

"Stop right there." The silver-haired lady held up a hand. "You know in my hands these knitting needles are lethal."

Max glared at wrinkled woman. "Take off that costume. Show me your face. Your real face."

Grandma regarded him with droopy eyes. After a moment of thought, she pinched her life-alert bracelet. The skin melted away like an ice-cream cone in a heat-advisory. As it ran down her neck and into her frumpy dress, it revealed the young face of a boy.

"Mandrake Mandrake," Max stepped back, stunned. He peeled back a curtain and spied out the front window. "So is this some kind of trap? Is the house surrounded?"

"If it was, I certainly wouldn't say." Mandrake wiped the melted skin-goo on the dress.

"I suppose not," Max laughed. "But it isn't a trap, is it?"

"Don't let the doilies and glass figurines fool ya," Mandrake folded his hands. "Crash Brickfist lives here now. His apartment wasn't big enough for two of us."

"But he's not part of this. He would never let you be bait." Max lifted a hideous ceramic horse from a bookshelf and pondered the extent Mindy had gone in order to keep this ruse up.

"No. Crash thinks I'm over at a friend's house. I asked the Seven to keep Mindy's secret a secret... until we knew for sure —"

"She didn't survive, then?" Sadness washed over Max.

Mandrake had to look away. "She took an impossible fall."

Max frowned. "So what's this about? How do you intend to stop me? You packing heat?"

Mandrake chuckled. "I'm afraid my skill with firearms is about as good as my knitting." He set the yarn and needles beside his feet. "I've been wondering why you escaped from prison after all this time. You had years of being in a Maximum Security prison and you didn't leave. Child's play for you. Even the Inspector's Crime Island wouldn't pose much of a challenge for a man who makes the impossible possible... so why now?"

"You're the one with all the answers," Max said.

"Mindy," Mandrake tapped the envelope. "You stayed in that prison, because somehow you think you deserved it."

Max frowned. "You're not as good as I thought."

"And you're not as bad. The first step in deciding between good and evil is knowing the difference."

Max laughed. Hard. "So what? You want me to return to crime fighting?"

"It's a thought. The world's worst villains are loose. The city is faced with its biggest challenge since... well... you... perhaps it's the type of challenge that stokes your fires?"

"So a team up? Father and son—"

"It's an option."

"What makes you think an old dog like me can change his ways?"

"Gran—" Mandrake stopped halfway through, restarted, "My mother. From what I can see, everything changed for her because of one single event—"

"Her treachery?"

"No... the birth of her son. She gave up everything she was... because of that one thing... and it all started with a single choice... a choice to do the right thing."

Max grunted. "No. She made a decision to betray the one she loved... then was exiled to a life of knitting and hiding."

"Rule number twenty-three – if it starts getting too personal, you may be missing clues."

"You'll make a fine adversary. Might even make things fun again." Max nodded to the envelope. "You read that... you'll change your mind about... Grandma."

"I doubt it," Mandrake said. "That's the past. I know who she was... who she is."

Max turned. "Well, then. I'll see you around, Detective." And with that, Max disappeared into the shadows.

As he slipped away from the house he caught a glimpse of his son, throwing the manuscript into the fireplace.

Nothing says "Happy Thirteenth" like Peckinpah's Gun Range and Rib Shack.

MANDRAKE'S NEW LEGAL GUARDIAN, Crash Brickfist, had taken it upon himself to impart those important 'father-son' lessons — kicking in doors, shooting guns, and BBQ. So when Mandrake found the neatly wrapped box on his pillow, he wasn't all that shocked to unwrap a .45 Colt Special with shoulder holster.

Mandrake raised his lethal new birthday gift and took aim downrange at the standard issue human silhouette target, as he mentally repeated the mantra Crash had imparted to him. "Clear your mind. Focus on the target."

In the six weeks since Crime Island collapsed, Mandrake's mind was clear as mud. The divers had failed to recover Grandma's (or Mindy's) body . Mandrake still remained optimistic. Unfortunately, his positivity fueled his hurt. Instead of moving on, every day hope lingered. He'd play the scene in his head over and over, searching for clues to her ultimate fate and debating what he might have done differently.

There were things he needed to tell her. Important things. He so wished he told her how much he loved her in the moments before the steel cables gave way and she dove into the turbulent waters below. One thing was for certain: he may be a boy detective, but he was no longer a child.

PA-KAW! Mandrake fired an errant shot. His wild recoil knocked him to the ground. He slowly opened his eyes to a shattered fluorescent light and Crash's meaty hand offering to help him up.

"Well, at least you hit something this time." Crash yanked him to his feet.

"Crash, I don't think I'm really a gun-type." Mandrake said.

"Maybe we could get you a crossbow or a flamethrower," Crash said carefully, putting the gun away. "We'll worry about that later. Right now, I have a surprise. A special guest. I think you're going to like this."

Hope surged through Mandrake. He turned as the door crept open on its own.

Mandrake beamed. He ran to the door and called out, "Mom!"

BOOM! An explosion erupted!

A wild boy spastically leapt through.

The Great Bill-O-Ni.

His cape was on fire.

Again.

The boy magician stomped on the flames. "I gotta invest in a fire-proof cape."

As the smoke cleared it revealed two other visitors — Ox and Abbey.

Abbey brought a cake baked to perfection. He knew it must be Abbey-made.

Ox presented him with a six-pack of STANK BODY ODOR FOR MEN.

Billy made balloon animals.

Crash ducked out around the time the pointy-hats and horns made an appearance. There were some lines grizzled street sleuths couldn't cross.

This gave Abbey and Mandrake time to talk privately.

"What's new with The Sleuthing Seven?" Mandrake asked as he dug into a small ice cream cup.

"Times are tough." Abbey put down her corner-piece of cake. She only ate the icing anyway. "The Seven's not a secret anymore. They're a target now. And the city is besieged by the world's worst villains. Not just the ones that escaped, either. The police department couldn't handle the crime wave. They quit. All of them."

"I saw that on the news." Mandrake twirled his spoon in his vanilla-chocolate swirl, drilling a hole to the bottom.

Abbey shook her head. "Without a police force every crook in the world has come to Capital City. It's like a playground for crime."

"I need to get back in. I need to help."

"Pinot thinks it's too dangerous under the circumstances." Abbey pulled an envelope with a red bow out of her bag. "But there might be something else."

Mandrake took the large package wrapped in sturdy paper. "It's not more STANK is it?"

"Just open it." She went back to her cake, letting him do the honors.

Mandrake tore it open. Inside was a book. The Inspector Strikes Back: A Villain's Manifesto!

"So this was what he was working on?" Mandrake stared into the monocled face adorning the cover.

"Self-published," Abbey smirked. "With lots of typos. He's forming a new super crime team. Word is, they're planning something big. Maybe you can dig in. Figure out where he might strike."

Mandrake tapped the cover of the book. "Of course."

"I gotta run. I'm practicing my parallel parking. I get my driver's license in a week." She stood, taking her piece of cake for the road.

"Hey Abbey, thanks for this."

"What're friends for?" She smiled and shuffled out the door.

Friends. He grinned to himself. She actually admitted it.

He had friends. Just like Grandma had always wanted for him.

As Mandrake reflected on his adventure, he realized sleuthing wasn't his only special talent. He was good at recognizing potential. What the world dismissed as snobby mean-girls or bullies or audio visual con-men, he saw as heroes. Even the Inspector wasn't a lost cause, even Mandrake's father.

Mandrake tucked the memoir inside his backpack and retrieved the ragged piece of notebook paper he snatched from Max Mandrake's cell. He gazed at the hand-written copy of the Rules of Amateur Sleuthing. He pulled out a pen and uncapped it. At the bottom of the list, Mandrake added a new rule, a rule that was now more important than the rest, a rule that would lead him to a new and dangerous case that would change everything forever.

Rule #45: Even the most hardened criminal has good in them... they just need a reason.

ABOUT THE AUTHOR

JAMIE NASH is a writing fool. *Emphasis on fool.* He writes for grownups and for TV and movies and books and comics. He's worked on movies for Nickelodeon like Tiny Christmas and Santa Hunters. He also co-wrote the book **BUNK!** He writes a lot of really scary horror movies too. Right now, he's busy typing up new stories in his hometown of Ellicott City, MD.

Want more?
Check out his website *www.jamienash.net*

Follow Jamie:
On Twitter — *@Jamie__Nash*
On Facebook — *@Jamie Nash – Writer*

CPSIA information can be obtained
at www.ICGtesting.com
Printed in the USA
LVHW091536011019
632855LV00004B/702/P

9 780999 091395